*Brett gave the hotel bed
a disgusted look,*

knowing he wouldn't be able to sleep. His bed at the ranch was big and wide, and suddenly he pictured her in it, her soft dark hair spread across his pillow while she slept. He shook his head to dislodge the picture, but it remained with him, and more disturbing images joined it: of long winter nights, of making love to her in that bed.

He scowled. He wasn't going to let her get to him like that. He'd take her and then forget about her, because in the taking he'd find that she was just like all the other women he'd had and then forgotten.

She had to be.

Dear Reader:

Nora Roberts, Tracy Sinclair, Jeanne Stephens, Carole Halston, Linda Howard. Are these authors familiar to you? We hope so, because they are just a few of our most popular authors who publish with Silhouette Special Edition each and every month. And the Special Edition list is changing to include new writers with fresh stories. It has been said that discovering a new author is like making a new friend. So during these next few months, be sure to look for books by Sandi Shane, Dorothy Glenn and other authors who have just written their first and second Special Editions, stories we hope you enjoy.

Choosing which Special Editions to publish each month is a pleasurable task, but not an easy one. We look for stories that are sophisticated, sensuous, touching, and great love stories, as well. These are the elements that make Silhouette Special Editions more romantic...and unique.

So we hope you'll find this Silhouette Special Edition just that—*Special*—and that the story finds a special place in your heart.

The Editors at Silhouette

SERL-7/85

LINDA HOWARD
The Cutting Edge

Silhouette Special Edition

Published by Silhouette Books New York

America's Publisher of Contemporary Romance

SILHOUETTE BOOKS
300 E. 42nd St., New York, N.Y. 10017

Copyright © 1985 by Linda Howington

Distributed by Pocket Books

ISBN: 0-373-09260-1

First Silhouette Books printing September 1985

10 9 8 7 6 5 4 3 2 1

America's Publisher of Contemporary Romance

Printed in the U.S.A.

LINDA HOWARD

says that books have been the ruling interest of her life. She began writing her own at the age of nine, but waited years before submitting one to a publisher. She has since sold that one and many more, and we at Silhouette Books are proud to present her work to you.

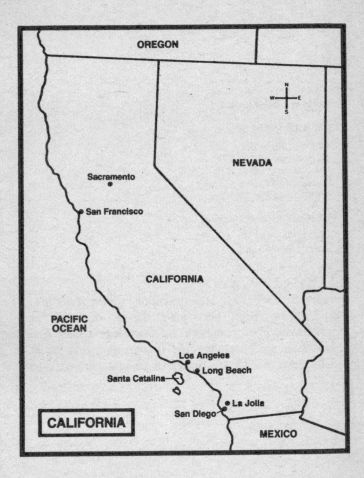

Chapter One

"That," said Brett Rutland in a quietly appreciative voice, "should be illegal."

Evan Brady had been watching the young woman who had just walked past them, too, and he could only agree. He'd already been in the Los Angeles office for a week, and he'd seen her several times. "You'll have to get in line, along with the rest of us," he advised Brett dryly. "Her social life would make a Philadelphia debutante green with envy."

A cool, hard smile touched Brett's lips. "Sorry; I think I'll cut in and go to the head of the line."

Evan was a little startled, for he'd never known Brett to become involved with anyone in the company before, and he'd really only been teasing. Still, when a man looked at Teresa Conway, other considerations tended to fly right out of his mind. Then he shrugged. "She doesn't look like the general idea of a bookkeeper, does she?"

Brett's dark blue eyes cut sharply to him. "Bookkeeper?"

"And damned good at what she does, too. She has to automatically be considered a suspect."

Brett nodded, turning his gaze once again to the slim back of the woman and watching until she entered the elevator and he was no longer able to see her. He and Evan were in Los Angeles to quietly investigate the mysterious discrepancy that an internal audit had turned up in the Los Angeles office of Carter Engineering, which was under the corporate umbrella of the Carter-Marshall Group. When Joshua Carter had heard of the possible embezzlement in his base company, he'd been livid, and Joshua Carter in a rage was something to behold, even though he was now pushing seventy. He'd called in his prize troubleshooter to investigate and handle the problem, and he'd instructed Brett to prosecute to the full extent of the law. Nobody stole from Joshua Carter and got away with only dismissal and a slap on the wrist! Bad publicity could go hang, for all he cared.

Brett shared with Joshua Carter the same cold distrust for a thief; he'd worked too hard to achieve his success to feel anything but contempt for anyone who tried to do it the easy way, by stealing the fruit of someone else's labors. It might take a while, but he and Evan would find the thief, and their handling of the situation would make everyone else in Carter Engineering think twice before they took so much as a pencil home.

Computer theft, by someone who really knew computers, could be a real bitch to track down, but Brett had full confidence in Evan's skills. There were few other people in the United States who could match Evan's expertise with a computer. With Evan working on the technical end, and Brett investigating the people, they'd have this wrapped up before the thief even knew they were coming. The cover story that had been given out was that they were in Los Angeles to investigate the feasibility of a new computer system that was being considered. Evan could make that look legitimate for an indefinite length of time.

Brett rubbed his jaw consideringly. "Do you know her name?" he asked Evan in an almost absent manner.

"Every man in this building knows her name," Evan replied, grinning. "Teresa Conway, but everyone calls her Tessa. She isn't married; I...uh, pulled her personnel file."

"Interesting reading?"

"Depends on what you're looking for. No obvious skeletons in her closet, though."

"I think I'll combine business with a little pleasure, and take Miss Conway out to dinner," Brett drawled.

"I'll pump her for information on the rest of the department; she may know of someone with financial problems, or have noticed any sudden riches."

"I hate for you to have to work so hard." Evan lifted his eyebrows sardonically. "I'll pull night duty for you and take the lady out, so you can get a good night's rest."

In admirably succinct language, Brett told him what he could do with his suggestion, and Evan grinned. He was thin and dark and intense, and he'd never suffered from a lack of female companionship. Probably he would have asked Tessa Conway out himself before the assignment was finished, but he'd been too busy and now Brett was stepping in, which meant that no one else would have a chance with her until Brett decided to walk away. Women didn't deny Brett Rutland; nature had given him a burning sexuality, a rawly demanding virility that drew women like moths to a candle, but his physical appetites were tempered by the icy control of his brain. Evan had never met a man more in control of himself than Brett Rutland.

Joshua Carter couldn't have picked a better choice than Brett to send in; he was cool, alert, and he didn't become emotionally involved. Evan had heard it said that Brett Rutland didn't give a damn about anyone, and on occasion he'd thought that the rumor just might be right. The clarity of Brett's thought processes was never clouded by sentiment or emotion. He had a guarded personality; he kept his thoughts well hidden, though most people never realized that, because he was so adept in handling them and bending them to his will.

"When we get back from lunch, I want to read her file," Brett said now. His navy blue eyes were intent, and Evan felt a moment's pity for Tessa Conway; she didn't have a chance.

As Tessa reentered the building after lunch, she smiled at the security guard at the front door, earning an ear-to-ear grin from him and an exasperated snort from Martha "Billie" Billingsley, who worked in the payroll department of Carter Engineering and who was also Tessa's closest friend.

"You'd flirt with a dead man," Billie growled.

"I wouldn't," Tessa defended herself good-naturedly. "Besides, there's a difference between flirting and just being friendly."

"Not where you're concerned, there isn't. You have every man in this building falling all over himself whenever you're anywhere near."

Tessa laughed, not taking Billie's charge at all seriously. She was a cheerful flirt, laughing and teasing, but doing it so lightheartedly that it was almost impossible not to laugh with her. Most people liked Tessa—even women—because she wasn't a poacher, despite the sunny charm that drew men to her like iron filings to a magnet. She was always the first person invited to a party because she was so lively. She had a sharp but kind wit, the sort that had people hanging on her lazy words, waiting with almost painful anticipation for her to get to the punch line, then exploding with mirth when she finally got it all said. Tessa's drawl would have driven everyone crazy months ago if the lazy music of it hadn't been so distracting. She was originally from Mobile, on Alabama's Gulf Coast, and Billie had long ago concluded that it would take an earthquake to make Tessa hurry. It was really odd how she managed to accomplish so much on her job, because she approached it with such calm laziness, never appearing ruffled or frantic no matter what crisis was crashing down on the office. Tessa just sort of strolled around, and things somehow got done. It was a complete mystery.

They entered the elevator, where they were joined by the company's computer genius, Sammy Wallace. Sammy was tall and thin and blond, with vague, sweet blue eyes behind horn-rimmed glasses that made him look like even more of a genius. Put him at the keyboard of a computer and he could practically make it sing opera, but he was almost painfully shy. Tessa felt protective of him, even though he was actually a few years older than she, and she greeted him warmly. He still blushed whenever she spoke to him, but he'd learned that the kindness in her eyes wasn't a lie, and he returned her smile. He might usually have his mind on computers, but he'd noticed how men looked at Tessa, and he felt a little proud that she always spoke to him.

"Do you have a free night for another chess lesson?" she asked, and he blushed a little more at the way she suggested that his social life was so busy that his free nights were few and far between. He liked that, and he gave her his sweet smile.

"How about tomorrow night?"

"Wonderful!" She rewarded him with a dazzling smile, her deep green eyes sparkling. "About seven?"

"Sure. Do you want to play poker again, too?"

"Now, you know I never turn down a poker game." She winked at him, and Sammy winked back, surprising even himself. He was teaching Tessa chess, and in return she was teaching him poker. He was so good with numbers that he was picking up the basics of poker far more easily than she was handling chess. Tessa played chess with verve and dash, going on instinct rather than strategy, and the board was often chaotic before her adversary figured out what was going on and began methodically boxing in her king. On the other hand, she was very good at poker; she liked the sheer exhilaration of blending skill and luck.

The elevator stopped at the next floor, and several men entered; Tessa moved toward the rear, holding the rail as the doors closed and they all moved upward again. It was lucky that she did hold on to the rail; when the elevator reached the next floor, it lurched violently before shuddering to a stop. Ted Baker, the man standing in front of her, lost his balance and flailed wildly in an effort to keep from falling. He succeeded, but his elbow crashed against Tessa's cheekbone, and she staggered from the force of the blow. Instantly, the man beside her had his arm around her waist, holding her up, and he swore softly.

The man who had hit her turned around, apologizing profusely. "It wasn't your fault," Tessa tried to reassure him.

"Baker, have a repairman called to check out the elevator," the man holding Tessa ordered, and Baker quickly murmured an acknowledgment.

Tessa had already recovered from the brief dizziness caused by the blow, and she tried to move away from the man, but he held her firmly within the hard circle of his arm. Billie squeezed over to them, her eyes anxious. "Tessa? Are you all right?"

"Yes, I'm fine." But she probed her cheekbone gingerly with her fingers, not certain if she was being truthful or brave. Her face felt a little numb.

"I'll take her up and put ice on it," the authoritative voice above her head said, and she doubted if anyone ever disobeyed that note of command. Certainly no one in the elevator made any other suggestion. Billie got off at their floor, looking back worriedly at Tessa, but she didn't try to accompany them. Little by little the elevator emptied as it rose higher and higher in the building, and Tessa pursed her lips thoughtfully at what that meant. She wanted to tilt her head back and get a good look at her rescuer, but he was standing slightly behind her, and she really didn't feel safe in moving her head that much. Sensation was returning to her face, and her cheekbone was throbbing painfully.

They exited on the executive floor, where Tessa had been only a few times in the past, since there was seldom any need for someone from bookkeeping to venture that far afield. He opened a door that had no name on it, but a secretary sprang to attention at her desk.

"Helen, do I have any ice in my office? There's been a slight accident."

"Yes, sir, I'm certain you do." Helen jumped to open the door for him, then walked straight to the small built-in bar in the corner of the large office to check the supply of ice. "Yes, there's ice. Do you need anything else?"

"I'll get a towel from my washroom," he said easily. "That'll be all, thanks."

The secretary left, closing the door behind her, and Tessa was alone in the big office with a man she'd never seen before. "Sit here," he instructed, easing her into the huge leather chair behind the desk that stretched out like a football field. He turned away to fetch a towel from his private washroom, and Tessa promptly got to her feet, propelled by both curiosity and an instinctive wariness of a man so used to giving commands and having them obeyed. She walked to the wide windows and looked out at the almost endless vista of Los Angeles. She heard him when he came back into the office, but she didn't look around.

"I told you to sit down," he said abruptly to her back.

"Yes, you did," Tessa agreed in a mild voice.

After a moment, he walked over to the bar, and she heard the clink of ice cubes as he got them out. "I'd feel better if you sat down; that was quite a crack you took."

"I promise I won't faint." She could hear him approaching...no, the thick carpet muffled his footsteps. She *sensed* his movements, as if her skin had become acutely sensitive to him; she actually felt the warmth of his body as he came closer. Turning, she faced him for the first time.

While he'd been holding her so closely against his side, she'd noticed several things about him. The first was that he was very tall, probably six-four, and very strong. She was of medium height, but her build was delicate and graceful, and she'd had the feeling that he could have lifted her with one hand. The heat and power of his hard-muscled body had been almost over-powering. She'd also noticed his clean male scent, and felt the lean strength of his hands.

Now he stood before her, looking at her with narrowed, intent eyes, and Tessa looked back.

A curiously light-headed feeling began to creep over her, and she wondered for a moment if she might have a slight concussion; then she realized that she was holding her breath. She let it out in a soft sigh, still staring up at the hard, distinctly unhandsome, but remarkably sensual and arresting face. He had the most beautiful eyes she'd ever seen on anyone: navy blue eyes, fringed by thick dark lashes, a blue as pure and deep as she could ever imagine. His hair was tawny brown, with strands of gold running through it, and verging on shagginess. He looked hard and sensual and perhaps a little cruel, and Tessa couldn't look away from him.

His chin was a little too prominent, his jaw a little too long, his cheekbones a little too high and raw and hard; his nose could almost be called beaky. His features were so roughly hewn that he might even have been called homely if it hadn't been for the dark blue beauty of his eyes and the sensually chiseled perfection of his mouth. That mouth was positively wicked, and she stopped breathing again when she looked at it. His mouth was just the right size, neither too wide nor too small, and his lips were mobile and clear cut, with a small curl to them that could be either cynicism or amusement. It was the mouth of a man of wide and varied experience, a man who knew how to kiss, how to savor the taste of a woman's skin. Tessa found herself suddenly shaken by the compulsion to rise on her tiptoes and find out for herself just how well he could kiss.

Very gently, he put one finger under her chin and tilted her face to the light so he could examine her cheek. "You'll have a bruise," he told her, "but I don't think your eye will turn black."

"I hope not!"

Cautiously he placed the makeshift ice pack against her cheek, and Tessa reached up to hold it in place. Her hand touched his, and she noticed that his fingers were slightly rough, not the hands of a man who never did anything more strenuous than sign his name. He didn't drop his hand, but kept it under hers, and he looked down at her with such calm, self-confident awareness in his eyes that Tessa automatically wanted to put a safer distance between them. She was used to charming men so easily that it wasn't even a conscious effort, but it was a lighthearted charm, and she always danced away before emotions could become intense. She couldn't have said how she knew it, but every bone in her body, every fiber of her flesh, every instinct of her very female personality, recognized him as being more than she could handle. He wasn't a man of easy charm; he overwhelmed women with the intensity of his maleness. He wouldn't let the butterfly flit away after dancing tantalizingly before him; he would reach out and capture her, and hold her for as long as her beauty intrigued him. Tessa knew that she had to go, then, in order to protect her own best interests. But she didn't want to go, she thought wistfully. She wanted to stay near him....

Beneath all the light and laughter, Tessa had a strong streak of common sense, and it surfaced now. "Thank you for the ice," she murmured as she stepped away from him. "I'd better get back to my job before I'm fired for being late. Thanks again—"

"Stay," he commanded softly, and it was definitely a command, despite the evenness of his tone. "I'll call your department head and cover for you."

"That won't be necessary. I'm really all right, so I can go back to work."

"If you insist." His lids dropped lazily over his deep-sea eyes. "I'd like to talk to you, though, so I'll take you out to dinner tonight. Will seven-thirty suit you?"

"Whoa!" she said, startled. "I don't even know you!"

"That's easily remedied." He held out his hard, sun-browned hand. "I'm Brett Rutland, from Carter-Marshall."

Tessa's eyes widened fractionally. She'd heard the name so many times during the past week, and so many people seemed to be a bit cautious of him that she'd begun actually to believe all the things she'd heard about him. Just the rumor that he might descend on Carter Engineering had made a lot of people nervous. He must have arrived that morning. But he was still holding out his hand, and slowly Tessa put her hand out to clasp his. His fingers wrapped gently around hers, as if he were very aware of the difference between his strength and hers.

"Tessa Conway," she said as a self-introduction. "I work in the bookkeeping department."

He didn't release her hand. "Well, Tessa Conway, now you know who I am and I know who you are. Dinner?"

She eyed him warily for a moment; then her natural sense of humor began to surface. Was this man the ogre everyone had been telling horror tales about? He was no one's tame pussycat, that was for certain, but he didn't look as if he ate raw meat for breakfast, either. Teasing lights began to dance in her green eyes. "I'm not certain I'd be safe with someone known as the *Ax-Man*," she pointed out cheekily.

He threw back his head and laughed, a good, deep sound, and a warmth began to grow inside her. "Ax-Man? That's better than what I'd thought! But you won't have anything to worry about, Tessa Conway. I won't chop you up into little pieces."

No, but he was a man who could put a woman's emotions through the meat grinder. Just standing there in the office with him, Tessa could feel her heart beating a little faster, and the way her blood was humming through her veins made her feel warm all over. Temptation was weakening her because she really wanted to go with him, but she knew that the smartest thing to do would be to run, not walk, to the nearest cover.

"If we went out together, the grapevine would short-out from the overload of gossip. I really don't—"

"I don't give a damn about gossip, and neither do you." His fingers tightened over hers. "Seven-thirty?"

She looked up at him again, and that was a tactical error. With a low, musical laugh, she cast caution to the winds. "Make it six-thirty. I'm the original sleepyhead; if I don't get my eight hours, I'm incapable of functioning. During the week, I don't even stay out as late as Cinderella did, and we all know she was a party-pooper."

Brett veiled his eyes with his lashes, not letting her see the predatory gleam in them. He'd be glad to make certain she was home in bed at an early hour; letting her sleep was something else entirely. "I'll be there. Write down your address for me." He planned to read her file, and he could get her address from there, but she didn't need to know that.

Tessa held the cold compress in place with her left hand while she scribbled her address on a scrap of paper, along with her telephone number. Then she looked at him again, and shook her head a little. "I must be out of my mind," she murmured to herself, and walked quickly out of the office before he could somehow entice her to stay even longer.

Brett sat down at his desk and toyed idly with the scrap of paper that contained her address. That was just how he wanted her: out of her mind, totally senseless with the pleasure he intended to give her. He'd had a number of affairs, enough that the prospect of another woman in his bed should produce only a feeling of mild anticipation, but the way he felt could never be described as mild. Whatever it was about Tessa Conway, he wanted her. He couldn't really remember a woman he'd wanted whom he hadn't eventually gotten, and usually within a fairly short length of time. There was no reason for things to be any different with Tessa. He thought of the way she walked, her slender hips moving in a way that made sweat pop out on his forehead. It might take a while for him to tire of her.

"I'm an idiot," Tessa told herself over and over as she returned to her office, still holding the ice-filled towel to her bruised cheekbone. She'd actually agreed to go out with a man who occupied a rather high rung of the corporate ladder in her company, and that in itself could give birth to a bumper crop of gossip. Not only that, the man had a horrible reputation; whenever he appeared, people lost their jobs. "Ax-Man" was a singularly appropriate nickname. But all of that aside, he was also the sexiest man she'd ever seen, or imagined. It wasn't his looks particularly, though his eyes were almost stunning in their beauty. It was the way he looked at a woman, as if she were his for the taking, and as if he knew all sorts of delicious ways to do the taking, and would linger over every moment of it. The eyes of a rake...except that there was something cool and controlled in his gaze, too, as if he held a part of himself aloof, totally untouched by the heat of his own passion.

What was a woman supposed to do with a man who would want more of herself than she felt safe in giving? Her heart had never been broken, but it had been battered badly enough that she didn't want to risk her emotions again, especially with a man like Brett Rutland. He'd ignore the barriers of laughter and lighthearted teasing, knocking them aside to get to the woman behind them. Tessa loved flirting and partying; it was a lot of fun, and frequently made people feel better about themselves. But the thought of getting serious with anyone was a little scary, and she was very much afraid that keeping things cool with Brett Rutland was only a remote possibility.

After two broken engagements, Tessa no longer had so many stars in her eyes. She was optimistic and level-headed enough not to condemn all men because of two failed relationships, but she was also more cautious now in the way she handled romantic entanglements. She knew danger when she saw it, and that man flashed danger signals like a neon sign. So why was she tossing aside all caution now, agreeing to go out with him when she knew better?

"Because I'm an idiot," she muttered to herself as she sat down at her desk.

Perry Smitherman, head of the bookkeeping department, came out of his office and approached her small cubicle. His high forehead was knit in a perpetual frown. "Billie Billingsley called to say you'd had a small accident. Is everything all right?"

"Yes, I'm fine." Tessa removed the cold compress and explored her swollen cheekbone with a light, cautious touch. "How does it look?"

His frown pulled even tighter as he bent down and examined the bruise as thoroughly as he would check the books. "Painful," he finally pronounced. "Do you need to go home?"

Tessa concealed her startled laughter. "No, I'm able to work," she assured him demurely. Perry was a fuss-budget, but he was kindhearted enough, and she liked him, for all his fussy ways.

"Did you go to the infirmary?"

"No. Mr. Rutland took me up to his office and put this compress on it—"

"Brett Rutland?" Perry asked sharply.

"Yes, he was in the elevator—"

His high, white forehead began to glisten with sweat. "Did he ask you anything about the department? Did he say anything about going over the books?"

Anxiety was evident in his face and his raised voice. Soothingly, Tessa said, "Not a word. He simply got the ice from his bar and wrapped it in the towel."

"Are you certain? He never does anything without a reason. He can be subtle, when it suits him. I'm sure he's going to go over everything; but he'll ask around first, and try to find out if we're slack or careless in any way."

"You don't have anything to worry about; the department is in good shape, and you're a very competent manager."

"You never know," he said, wringing his hands. "You never know."

He was determined to think the worst, and with a sigh Tessa gave up the effort of cheering him; he was probably happier looking for a dark lining in a silver cloud anyway. Some people simply had a melancholy outlook, and Perry was one of them.

Billie popped in during the mid-afternoon break to check on Tessa. The other woman was full of curiosity about Brett Rutland, her big brown eyes even rounder than usual as she stared at Tessa and shot questions at her faster than they could be answered. "What did he say? How long did he keep you? Were you scared? My gosh, of all the people who could have been in that elevator! Did he say why he's here?"

Tessa picked out one question and ignored the others. "Why should I have been scared? I didn't know who he was."

Billie gaped. "You didn't know Brett Rutland?"

"I knew the name, but I'd never seen him, so how could I have known him?"

Looking impatient with such logic, Billie still tried to pry more information out of Tessa, who could be infuriatingly hard to pin down when she wanted to be. "What did you say? What did he say?"

"Among other things, he told me to sit down while he got a towel," Tessa murmured. She wasn't going to tell Billie that he'd asked her out to dinner; just the thought of going out with him affected her nerves, jarring her out of her usual lazy contentment and making her feel jittery, and both afraid and excited at the same time. She was still tingling from the sizzling electricity of his masculinity.

Aunt Silver would adore him.

Just the thought of her aunt made Tessa smile, because Silver was the warmest, liveliest, most lovable woman in existence, and if there was anything Silver appreciated, it was an exciting man. "Sugar," Silver had told her more than once, "if I ever stop man watching, you'll know to bury me, because that's a sure sign that I'm dead." Since Silver was prospering with her small, exclusive doll shop in Gatlinburg, Tessa was certain that her aunt was still happily man watching, too.

"You're smiling," Billie accused. "*Teresa Conway!* Don't you dare try flirting with that man! I know that look in your eyes; have you been batting your eyelashes at him?"

"With my face looking as if I'd just gone ten rounds with a heavyweight boxer?" Tessa asked in a mild voice.

"Would you let a little thing like that stop you?"

"I promise, I haven't been flirting with Mr. Rutland." Her eyes twinkled; evidently Mr. Rutland didn't wait for a woman to flirt with him before he made his move.

"I hope not! He's been known to tear strips of flesh off people who have looked at him wrong."

Several things about Brett Rutland alarmed Tessa, but not the fear that he'd tear strips of flesh off her. No, what he'd do to her flesh wouldn't be painful at all, and that inner certainty was probably the most alarming thing she felt about him. Whenever a woman looked at a man and knew, instinctively and without doubt, that he would be able to give her exquisite pleasure, her defenses against that man were dangerously weakened. Tessa didn't want her defenses to be weakened; she'd been hurt badly, not once but twice. Later, after time had completely healed all her emotional wounds, she wanted to try love again. But not now, she thought despairingly. I'm not ready now.

She managed to assure Billie that she hadn't done anything shocking that could cost her her job. Billie was an uneasy mixture of laid-back California casualness and a surprising streak of prudery that was frequently shocked by Tessa's flirtatiousness. Because she was also a loyal friend, Tessa looked out for Billie in subtle ways that no one had ever realized, though many thought that Billie had guided Tessa through the mazes and pitfalls of life in Southern California, where the normal flow of traffic was practically a death sentence for a young woman used to using a much more leisurely pace in getting from one place to another. Since Tessa had become Billie's friend, Billie's clothes had become simpler, more classic in style, and more suited to her short, rather rounded figure. Billie's hairstyle now flattered her face, her makeup accentuated her large brown eyes and camouflaged her rather sallow complexion. Before, Billie's taste in jewelry had run to heavy, clunky pieces in neon colors that had tended to make her look like a midget in the circus. Now she wore smaller pieces, well coordinated with her clothing. Billie's social life had picked up considerably in the last year, but she never wondered why. Tessa knew why, and the knowledge filled her with quiet satisfaction. She'd been lucky; she'd had Aunt Silver to guide her in her confusing teenage days, to teach her how to dress and use makeup; not many girls were so lucky. Spreading around a little of Aunt Silver's knowledge was the least she could do.

She'd have to remember to write to Aunt Silver about Brett Rutland; her aunt would definitely enjoy hearing about a man with navy blue eyes and a mouth that made a woman go a little crazy.

Brett leaned back in his chair, his eyes narrowed as he flipped through the scanty information in Tessa's personnel file. There wasn't a lot in there: She'd never been arrested, never been married and had no identifying scars or birthmarks. Her supervisor, Perry Smitherman, had given her a good evaluation, but Brett thought cynically that any normal man would find it difficult to say anything unfavorable about Tessa, even an old-maid type like Perry Smitherman.

He tossed the file onto his desk; its contents were useless. He'd find out more about her tonight.

Chapter Two

Tessa leaned closer to the mirror and examined her discolored, swollen cheekbone, then frowned. Her normal makeup hadn't covered the bruise as well as she'd hoped; she carefully applied a concealer, and blended it until she was satisfied that the bruise was hardly noticeable.

She'd gotten caught in the snarled traffic, and as a result had only arrived home a mere half an hour before, but the situation was well in hand. She'd plugged in her hot rollers, then stripped and taken a fast shower and washed her hair. By the time she'd blown her hair dry, the rollers were hot, and she'd set a few of them in her hair for lift and control. Makeup had taken an additional ten minutes. Now she took the rollers from her hair and deftly brushed it into a casually sophisticated style that swirled about her shoulders. A glance at the clock told her that she had twelve minutes left, ample time to get dressed.

Tessa disliked hurrying, but she seldom had to hurry, because she had everything organized. Organization was insurance against haste. She knew where everything was, and had her routine well planned; if circumstances conspired against her and she was thrown off schedule, she would hurry, if work were involved, but she never hurried for personal reasons. Oddly, she was almost never late, as if the little gremlins who disrupted schedules realized that they wouldn't get any satisfaction from watching her dash around madly, so they seldom bothered with her. At least, that was the explanation she'd worked out in her mind, and it suited her as well as any other.

She sprayed herself lightly with her favorite perfume, then put on her underwear, her hosiery and her dress. The dress was cream-colored silk, with a slim skirt and a wrap bodice, and long sleeves to keep her arms warm in the April night. She slipped pearl studs into her ears, then fastened a single long strand of creamy pearls around her neck. Pale beige sling-backs lifted her a few inches higher, giving her a willowy, swaying grace. Just as she picked up her matching beige evening purse, the doorbell rang, and she nodded in satisfaction. "Right on time," she told herself in congratulation, and she meant herself, not him.

She opened the door to him, and as soon as she met his dark blue eyes she felt a sudden rushing warmth inside. Darn, but the man packed a wallop! All he had to do was smile and a woman was reeling on the ropes. But none of what she felt was in her lazy smile as she invited him inside. "Would you like a drink before we go?"

"No, thanks." He looked around her small, cozy apartment, full of comfortable furniture and warm lighting, with her many unrelated collections filling every nook and corner. "Nice. It looks homey."

With some people, "homey" would have been a polite way of saying "cluttered," but somehow Tessa felt that he meant it. Andrew would have turned up his nose at the comfortable but definitely unfashionable decor, but then Andrew was very much concerned with keeping up his image. She sighed; she'd promised herself several times that she'd never think of Andrew again, but somehow he sneaked back into her mind at odd times. Why should she think of him now, when she was going out with a man who put Andrew completely in the shade? Perhaps her subconscious was dredging up Andrew's memory in an effort to put her on her guard and protect her against a man who was so much more dangerous than Andrew had ever been.

His car was a rental, but a luxury model for all that. She'd heard it said that Brett Rutland was Mr. Carter's fair-haired boy, and perhaps he was. After helping her into the car, he walked around to the driver's side and folded his long length behind the wheel. When she considered his height, she realized that he had to have a large car; a man with legs that long would never be comfortable in a sports model.

"I made reservations for seven o'clock," he said, and she caught a glint of amusement in his normally controlled expression. "You should be home by ten-thirty; can you stay awake that long?"

"I might," she drawled, not giving him an inch. A tiny smile tugged at the corners of his mouth.

"I'll try to make sure you stay awake," he said in a voice that almost purred with sensuality.

Oh, she'd just bet he would! Probably the only time any woman had gone to sleep on him was in his arms, after the loving was finished.

"What part of the South are you from?" he asked casually, as if he hadn't read her file.

"I was born in Mobile, Alabama. But when I was thirteen my mother and I moved to Tennessee to live with her sister." Those were the bare facts; they didn't tell of her mother's long battle with ill health, the poverty they'd endured, the times when there simply hadn't been anything to eat because her mother hadn't been able to work. Finally her mother had given up and swallowed her stubborn pride and asked her sister to drive down from Tennessee to get them, and even then she'd asked for Tessa's sake, not her own. It was just that her mother's entire family had been against Tessa's father, and they'd been proved right, for he'd walked out on his family when Tessa was too young even to remember him. Tessa's mother had lived barely a year after the move, and after that there'd been only Tessa and Silver in the old farmhouse just outside of Sevierville.

"What made you move out here?"

"I wanted to see something of the country," Tessa replied easily. She wasn't about to tell him about Andrew. She'd hated the idea of leaving, but Aunt Silver had talked her into it. She wasn't running, Aunt Silver had said; she was turning her back on a bad situation and walking away from it. Well, Andrew thought she'd run, but eventually Tessa had come to realize that what Andrew thought didn't matter worth a hoot. If only Andrew hadn't been a hot, rising young executive at the company where Tessa had worked!

"Do you like it?"

"Well enough. What about you? You have a bit of a drawl yourself, but I can't place it."

He looked surprised, as if she wasn't supposed to ask any of the questions. "I'm from Wyoming. My father and I own a ranch there."

"A real ranch? Don't you miss it?" Her eyes had brightened with interest, and she'd turned in her seat to face him, a movement that made the draped bodice of her dress gape open just a bit, enough to allow his quick glance to caress the soft, beginning curve of her breast.

He wanted to put his hand inside her dress and feel the satiny swell, to make her nipple pucker against his palm. The jolt of pure desire that hit him took him by surprise, and he had to force himself to concentrate on her question.

"Yes, I miss it." The admission surprised him, because he'd been ignoring the increasing need to walk away from the whole rat race and go back to what he'd grown up doing, ranching. Old Tom was proud of his son for making it big in the business world, and Brett had to admit that he'd enjoyed the challenge of it himself. But now...he was getting older, and so was old Tom, and when it came down to it there was nothing that gave him the satisfaction of a hard day's work in the saddle. He wondered what this soft, sleekly sophisticated creature beside him would say if he told her that more and more often he wanted to go home, to Wyoming and the growing Rutland spread.

"I'm going to go home, someday," she said softly. "This isn't going to be my permanent home. Home is an old farmhouse that needs a coat of paint, and a dilapidated barn behind it that even the old cow was afraid to go in." She laughed a little at her memories, but they were good, warm memories, because Aunt Silver had filled that old farmhouse with enough love to completely shelter her young, confused niece. Aunt Silver had left the old farm now, though she still owned it, and moved to a modern house in Gatlinburg, but Tessa meant to fix up the old farmhouse and live in it someday. The best times of her life had been spent there.

Looking at her now, Brett found it hard to believe that her childhood had been a deprived one. She looked as expensive as a woman from a moneyed, blue-blooded background, educated in a private school in Virginia. Why would she want to go back, if she had it so much better here?

Tessa thoroughly approved of the restaurant he'd chosen; she'd never been there before, but the interior was dim and the diners were all discreetly isolated, while the music was low and pleasant. They were shown to a private little alcove, where a candelabrum with three tall white tapers was the only light. The table was small, and she found that when they were seated their knees bumped. Their eyes met across the table, and a slow, sleepy smile touched his lips and made his eyelids droop heavily. He spread his legs until they were on either side of hers, then gently closed them so that his calves clasped hers. Her heartbeat bolted into a faster rhythm as she felt the warmth of his legs, the muscular strength of his calves. He'd have legs like a linebacker, she thought suddenly, and her legs felt burned from his heat.

Over a glass of very good wine, he continued questioning her, small, innocent questions that she answered willingly. She was too bemused by the possessive clasp of his legs to really pay any attention to the polite, getting-to-know-each-other questions that he gently posed to her every so often. Inevitably, they talked about work, since that was a common ground for them. He didn't seem to be digging for any dirt, and he was so knowledgeable about the firm anyway that she found herself telling him funny anecdotes about the people she worked with, nothing that would get anyone in trouble, but the humorous little things that happened to everyone. She didn't spare herself, either, and laughed as hard at the spots she'd gotten herself into as she did at any of the other stories. He countered with his own tales of the things that had happened to him during the years he'd been with Carter-Marshall, and Tessa completely relaxed.

Brett was too coolly controlled ever to be a social lion, but in a private situation with a woman he wanted, he was unrivaled. He charmed without threatening, making her feel appreciated without coming on too strong, skillfully wearing down any inner defenses. He wanted Tessa very much. It wasn't that she was the most beautiful woman he'd ever seen because she wasn't; but she was almost certainly the sexiest woman he'd ever met. It wasn't anything he could really put his finger on; she was slender rather than voluptuous, though very shapely indeed. But her soft green eyes sparkled with teasing amusement, and her wide, generous mouth was made for passion. Her dark brown hair looked like thick silk as it curled around her delicate shoulders. With those high, beautiful cheekbones, she looked exotic and a little foreign. She teased and flirted...oh, she had flirting down to a fine art. Every time her long dark lashes languorously swept down to veil the cheerfully wicked glint in her eyes, he felt his body tighten with need. She played at being the vamp, but she did it so boldly, laughing at herself and enjoying the role so much, that it was unbelievably effective. She invited everyone else to enjoy themselves as lightheartedly as she did, but she didn't seem to realize what a challenge she was. Brett thought of having her beneath him in bed, that full mouth no longer laughing but swollen from his kisses, and her sweet, satiny body accommodating his passions. He'd have to be gentle with her, at least at first, he thought as his eyes narrowed intently on her. She was delicately built, with slender, fragile bones.

Tessa looked up from the prime rib she was devouring with elegant greed, and found him watching her with sexual intent burning with obvious fire in his eyes. She went suddenly still, her mouth soft and a little tremulous. Without taking his eyes from her, he lifted his wineglass and drank the rich red liquid.

"Finish eating," he said gently.

"I can't." Despite the way he made her feel, so shaky inside, she smiled at him. "You're staring at me."

"I know. I was thinking how much I'd rather be having you than this roast beef."

His voice was so tender and low that it was a moment before she realized exactly what he'd said, and her eyes widened even more. She felt utterly hypnotized, sitting there and staring at him as helplessly as a rabbit must stare at a lion about to pounce. Giving herself an inner shake, Tessa gathered her senses. "Finish your roast anyway," she admonished him. "Aunt Silver always told me that the only thing worth betting on was a sure thing, so don't turn down your bird in the hand...or in this case, beef on the plate."

His hard mouth curved in amusement. "Do you really have an Aunt Silver, or do you just use the idea as a diversion?"

Feeling more on top of the situation again, Tessa gave him a look so innocent that it should have been patented. "Now, could I really make up an Aunt Silver?"

"If it suited you."

"You're probably right," she agreed comfortably, smiling at him. "But in this case, I don't have to rely on my imagination. Aunt Silver is my actual, living, breathing aunt."

"The one you and your mother went to live with?"

"Yes. Mother died not long after we moved to Tennessee, so Aunt Silver and I were closer than we'd normally have been. All we had was each other. She's fantastic; she's my aunt, my mother and my best friend all rolled into one."

"Does she still live in Tennessee?" That was another bit of information that he'd already gotten from her file, but Brett's cool attention to detail never faltered. He wanted her to give the details of her life herself, partly to account for the knowledge he already had, and also to give him the chance to see if she told it exactly as she'd put it in her file, or if she was reluctant to answer any personal questions. So far, she was an open, warmly responsive woman, and he wanted her more and more as the minutes passed.

"She owns a doll shop in Gatlinburg; she lives there now. The old farmhouse needs a lot of work done on it, and the only heat is the fireplace and old woodstove, so it was a lot easier on her just to move to Gatlinburg, as well as being safer during the winter. Now she doesn't have to drive on those icy roads." Tessa gave her slow smile. "I hope she'll close the shop for a couple of weeks of vacation this winter, during the slow season, and come out here to visit."

Brett's eyes sharpened with interest. "Slow season?"

"The Smoky Mountain park headquarters are in Gatlinburg. The summer months, and through October, are the busiest, though a lot of people go during the winter, too, for the snow."

He shook his head. Wyoming born and bred, he still couldn't understand why anyone would actually *want* snow. It seemed to him that every winter they'd always had more snow than anyone could want in a lifetime. He skied, and did it well, but he'd never been enthusiastic over the sport or the snow necessary for it. But more and more he found himself missing Wyoming, even those god-awful winters.

Tessa laughed at his expression. "Listen, when you live in the South, snow is rare. I'd never seen snow at all until we moved to Tennessee."

They finished their main courses, and the waiter promptly cleared the dishes away, while they lingered over the wine. Tessa had thought that she wouldn't be able to eat any dessert, but when the waiter brought the dessert cart, she stared at the scrumptious pastries until her mouth was watering. "I can't resist it," she sighed, choosing her dessert.

Brett declined a sweet, but they both ordered coffee, and he slowly drank his as he watched her attack the pastry. She certainly enjoyed her food, for someone so slim. She glanced up at him and caught his gaze, and smiled as she read his thoughts. No words were necessary; it was one of those strangely intimate interludes when two minds march together, and she felt closer to him at that moment than she ever had with anyone else.

His gaze lowered. "You have a crumb on your lip," he said softly, and Tessa ran her tongue slowly, searchingly, over her lips in quest of the errant crumb.

His navy eyes darkened to black. "You missed it. Lean over and I'll get it off for you."

Obligingly Tessa leaned over, smiling at him, so he could flick the crumb off with his finger. He paused for a moment, searing her with the dark heat of his gaze, then leaned over slowly, like a man moving at the command of a force stronger than he. As the distance between them lessened, Tessa's eyes widened until they were large green pools, soft and deep. Surely he wasn't going to kiss her, was he? Lightly his mouth touched her, found the crumb, and his tongue captured it. Tessa quivered under that light touch, filled with his taste, the heat and smell of his skin surrounding her. She felt almost paralyzed, totally unable to move away from him. She was as overwhelmed by him as if he'd put his arms around her and was holding her tightly to his lean, hard frame, though he'd touched her only with his mouth, and that so lightly and delicately that she'd scarcely been able to feel it.

He moved away, and the heat in his eyes had intensified, his gaze locked on her face. His expression hadn't changed, but Tessa's tingling nerve endings picked up the small, almost imperceptible signals of his growing arousal. His skin seemed to be pulled tighter over his fierce cheekbones; his lips were redder, a bit fuller. Tessa's body throbbed in rhythm with his thundering heartbeat, as if his body set the pace for hers. His heat lured her, pulling her closer.

"Are you ready to leave?" he asked, and his raspy voice was even rawer than usual.

Tessa had a mental image of herself cheerfully, blindly wading ever deeper into the dark sea of temptation. In over my head, she thought with faint despair, then threw caution to the wind and nodded. "Yes. I'd like to go home now, please."

He didn't even take her arm as they walked back out to his car, but tension vibrated between them. Tessa glanced up at his controlled face, wondering how a man with such steely self-control could at the same time project the raw, steamy sensuality that was overwhelming her own instinctive caution before he'd even made a real move toward her. That fleeting brush of lips in the restaurant hadn't qualified as a real kiss, but even that had sent rockets of pleasure zinging through her body.

She was a little stunned by the intensity of her feelings. Not even with Andrew had she *wanted* so badly, and she'd loved Andrew. Nor had she been physically attracted to Will, but Will had been an infatuation, not love. She was accustomed to attracting men; it was effortless on her part, and she simply accepted it as part of her personality. She kept it light, enjoying herself and enjoying the knowledge that the men in her life had *fun* when they were with her. Life was for laughter, for teasing and joking and dancing, for feeling good. It was for love, too, but she knew that love didn't come as easily as laughter.

Tessa was a creature made for the sunlight, warm and bright; the man beside her was controlled, even a little grim, though she'd been able to bring the light of laughter to his eyes several times. For all the warm golden streaks in his hair, for all the heat of his sexuality, he was a man who held himself aloof mentally, whose emotions were cool and even. But he made her heart jump at the sight of him, as no other man had ever done. He made her ache, as if she were suddenly incomplete, and yearning to be a part of a whole, with him.

What if I fall in love with him? she thought in sudden panic, and looked at him with apprehension plain in her eyes. He wasn't like other men; with him, she wouldn't be able to control the relationship as she'd always done before. He would take everything she had to give, all of the sunlight and sweet secrets, and she wasn't certain that he would give her anything in return. Oh, she knew that he was physically attracted to her, but he kept his emotions, his thoughts, carefully shielded. She was totally uncertain of herself in that regard, and she wasn't used to feeling as if she was walking in emotional quicksand.

Brett had seen the brief moment of fear that had glimmered in her eyes, and he wondered what had caused it. What was she afraid of? She certainly wasn't afraid of him as a man; she was too damned enticing and flirtatious. His brows pulled together in a momentary frown, before he smoothed them again. He'd solve all her riddles, eventually.

As he pulled the car to the curb at her apartment, he glanced at his wristwatch. "Ten o'clock, Cinderella. You're safe for the night."

She chuckled, then quickly sobered. Was she safe? She wasn't certain yet, and she wouldn't be until she'd seen him on his way. What if he wanted to stay? She'd already learned that her toughest problem with controlling him would be controlling herself. If he could make her melt with a barely-there kiss, what would she do if he turned his charm on full power?

His hand rested lightly on the small of her back as they went up the walk, but even that touch affected the rhythm of her heartbeat. "Let me have your key," he murmured. She got it from her purse and gave it to him. He unlocked the door, then stepped inside the apartment before she could think of a way to keep him from coming in. She stood just inside the door and watched as he turned on the lights and checked all the rooms. "All secure," he said, smiling a little.

"Is this security check standard?" she asked, curiosity momentarily taking her attention.

His eyes were like the deep Pacific, with golden lights dancing on top of the blue waves. "Yes," he said simply, and came over to her where she still stood by the door. Taking her arm, he drew her farther inside and pushed the door closed. He cupped her face in his hard, warm hands, turning it up and studying the generous mouth, the languid sweep of her thick dark lashes. It was a passionate face for all its delicacy, and he wanted the taste of her mouth on his.

She clasped her hands around the thickness of his wrists, and he felt the faint quiver of her body. Without a word, he bent his head and covered her lips with his mouth, feeling the sweet softness tremble and part, and he kissed her harder, tilting her head back even more so he could slant his mouth across hers and deepen the caress. Tessa helplessly opened her mouth to his tongue. No man should taste this sweet and heady, but he did, and she cried a little inside because she was afraid he would hurt her if she gave him any opening into her emotions, but she was also afraid that she wouldn't be able to protect herself.

He lifted his mouth from hers a fraction of an inch, and his wine-sweet breath wafted over her lips as he demanded in a low, harsh voice, "Kiss me the way I'm kissing you. Give me your tongue. I want it now; I want you to kiss me the way I know you can." Almost fiercely, he put his mouth over hers again, and with a little sigh Tessa gave in to the delicious, erotic demand. She kissed him as if he were hers, as if she had every right to him, every right to demand everything from him. With her lips and tongue she claimed him, kissing him deeply, forgetting the need to protect herself. His frank, heated sensuality overcame the barriers of laughter that she used to keep people from becoming too intimate, and tapped into the deep, passionate core of her womanhood. Tessa was a woman with a deep reservoir of love and passion waiting to be given to the one man who would be the love of her life. She knew the worth of her love; she wasn't about to waste it on a casual, fly-by-night relationship no matter how attractive the man. Always before, she'd been able to keep the necessary mental control to ensure this, but now she felt her control slipping away, felt herself giving him the first taste of the searing magic of her passion.

His hands left her face; one arm went around her rib cage, locking her to him with a steely strength that made her shiver as she realized how very strong he was. His other hand went to the back of her head and seized a handful of hair, exerting just enough pressure to hold her head back without hurting her. He lifted his mouth from hers again, and his breathing was ragged, his eyes burning with need.

Tessa quivered against him, well aware of his need; pressed against him as she was, she could feel every taut line of his body. She knew that she should say something light, something to make him laugh, to break the mood, but she couldn't seem to think of anything very effective. "Was that what you wanted?" she finally managed, but her voice was so low and whispery with her own need that the words were more of an invitation than the light mockery she'd intended.

"That was part of it," he said in rasping admission, and began kissing her again. Her senses noticed the roughness of his voice, and she knew the more aroused he became, the lower and rougher his voice was, until he spoke in little more than a growl. She clung to his heavy shoulders, helplessly giving his mouth everything it sought, the freedom and depth and response of her own mouth. He was teaching her the power of physical desire, making her want him in a way she'd never wanted a man before, so deeply and powerfully that it was becoming desperation.

In Brett's experience, the unguarded response she was giving him meant that she was his for the taking. Though his loins were throbbing heavily, his mind was cool as he deliberately put his hand inside the wrap bodice of her dress, cupping the warm silk of her breast in his palm and discovering with delight that the curves of her breasts were lusher than he'd expected, given her almost fragile slenderness. His slightly rough thumb moved over the velvet nipple, gently turning it into a firm, impudent little nub.

Tessa jerked away from him.

Her instinctive action startled her as much as it did him. She blinked in bewilderment, then stared at him as she wasn't quite certain what had happened. Her eyes were enormous, her face a little pale. "I wasn't expecting that," she said a little helplessly.

Brett ground his teeth in mingled rage and frustration. His entire body ached; his hands twitched, wanting the sweetness of her flesh beneath his fingers again. "Damn you, I ought to—" he began gutturally, then stopped before he said too much, before his male frustration led him to say things he didn't mean. He meant to see her again, even if tonight wasn't ending the way he'd planned. He'd have her yet, and he also thought he might be able to get more information about her fellow employees from her.

Tessa pressed shaking fingers to her mouth. "I know. I'm sorry," she said weakly. "I never meant to let things...that is, you startled me when you touched...oh, damn it."

He looked at her sharply. She was visibly trembling, and something very like fear was in those wide eyes as she stared at him—fear like he'd seen before, during dinner, and he felt a sudden, keen curiosity. No, he had to reassure her, calm her down so she wouldn't refuse to see him again.

He took a deep breath to calm the ragged pace of his breathing, and to bring his voice back to normal. "It happened too fast, didn't it?" he asked quietly.

Tessa brought herself back under control, too. "I'm not a tease, but I don't sleep around either. I don't believe in casual encounters. We just met today, after all. I didn't mean to let this happen."

"I understand." He managed a smile, a brief, grim smile. "Not that I think there would be anything casual about our encounter. We'd probably blow the needle off the Richter scale."

Tessa had thought herself long past the blushing stage, but the color that rose to her cheeks was from excitement, not embarrassment. He was looking at her in a way that almost scorched her, and the painful part of it was that she still wanted him, too, in just the way he was imagining. Her body had reacted instinctively, independent of her mind and common sense, and her flesh had recognized him immediately as a worthy partner.

"Tomorrow night. Dinner again."

She couldn't take her eyes from him. "I can't. Sammy Wallace is trying to teach me how to play chess."

Brett remembered overhearing her make the date in the elevator, and his almost photographic memory dredged up an image of Sammy Wallace: thin and blond and no match at all for this sweet little Southern Delilah.

"All right," he allowed grimly. "The night after, then. And don't tell me no."

"I wasn't going to." Never off stride for long, Tessa felt enough like herself to give him her slow-breaking smile that held him breathless as he watched the beginning curve of her lips and waited for the smile to reach full bloom. "I must have more courage than brains."

He didn't feel like smiling, but the twinkle in her eyes invited him to share in the laughter at herself. He didn't want to laugh; he wanted to take her to bed, and the coiled tension in his body told him that he'd have to take a cold shower before he could sleep. "I'll see you Thursday night. Six-thirty?"

"Yes, that's fine."

He'd turned to the door, but he paused and glanced back at her, his face grim. "This Sammy Wallace, is he special to you?"

"He's a very sweet and very shy man, and he's also a genius. He's teaching me chess." Why was she explaining herself to him? But from the way he was looking at her, he didn't think that was explanation enough.

"Don't make any more dates with him, or with anyone else except me."

The possessive order made her eyes widen. "Are you going Neanderthal on me?" she asked suspiciously.

"If I have to. You shouldn't have kissed me the way you did if you didn't want me to lay claim." Very calmly, he caught her chin in his hand and kissed her, slow and hard. "Remember that."

When he was gone, Tessa creamed off her makeup and brushed her hair, then pulled on her light nightgown and tumbled into bed. She was a hard sleeper; nothing interfered with her rest, and tonight was no exception. She went immediately to sleep, but her subconscious played the night for her again and again in dreams that didn't stop with the touch of his hand on her body.

Evan's eyes were tired and red-rimmed from the work he'd been doing at night as well as the bogus work necessary during the day, but his mind was still running at full speed. He was totally caught up in their covert search for the embezzler. "Did you get any useful information from Miss Conway last night?" he asked absently when Brett entered the office.

"I've made notes," Brett answered, taking a small notebook from his inside coat pocket. The details he'd noted were insignificant, except to himself and Evan. He'd had to be careful in his questioning, since Tessa wasn't a gossip, but he'd gotten a surprising amount of information from her humorous tales.

Evan read the notes, frowning as he added the information to the profiles he was compiling on each employee under suspicion, which was, at that point, virtually everyone.

"What do you have on Sammy Wallace?" Brett asked slowly, frowning at himself for asking the question. He didn't like the possessive jealousy he was feeling; he'd never felt it for any woman before, and he didn't want to feel it now.

Evan's head snapped up. "He's a computer genius," he said slowly. "He has a system at his apartment that the CIA could use. From what I've found so far, he has to be the prime suspect. What made you ask?"

Brett shrugged, his eyes intent. If Wallace was the prime suspect, he'd make damned sure Tessa didn't have anything else to do with him.

Chapter Three

All day long, Tessa had looked forward to Sammy's undemanding company as an antidote against the tension that curled in her stomach at just the thought of Brett Rutland, and Brett had occupied her thoughts so much that day that she wondered if she'd made a mess of everything she'd done.

"Aunt Silver, you never warned me about men like him," she grumbled aloud, as if her aunt were in the room with her instead of almost an entire continent away. "I think I've met the man I could really love, but it's not safe to love him. He's a real heartbreaker. So what now?"

Take it as it comes.

That was exactly what Aunt Silver's answer would be. She was a wonderfully romantic woman, but soundly based in common sense. Silver had probably faced the same dilemma when she met the man who would eventually be her husband. From what she'd heard from both her mother and Silver, Tessa had surmised that her uncle had been as wild as a mink, with charm to burn and an itch for Silver that Silver had been determined he wasn't going to scratch. Their running battle had lasted for almost two years and kept three counties enthralled, wondering who would win. Silver had won, and their marriage had been as temptestuous and as loving as their courtship. It must run in the family for the women to fall in love with rakes and rascals, she thought.

"I won't fall in love with him!" Tessa said fiercely as she took the stairs up to Sammy's apartment, then admitted to herself that she was whistling in the dark.

When he answered the door, Sammy's face was flushed with excitement and his hair was mussed. "Tessa, just wait until you see the new computer we've put together! It's a real honey."

Tessa was thoroughly familiar with computers, but only from a user's standpoint. She knew absolutely nothing about microchips or interfacing, and wasn't interested in learning, but she smiled at the enthusiasm on Sammy's face. "Tell me about it," she invited.

"See for yourself. Hillary's here, too."

Tessa had never met Hillary before, but Sammy had often talked about her. Hillary lived on the floor above him, and she was as wild about computers as he was. Tessa supposed it was a case of kindred spirits. The young woman she saw seated at the display terminal and practically attacking the keyboard only reinforced that original supposition, for Hillary was as blond as Sammy. Her slim figure was encased in jeans and a jersey, and her long blond hair was pulled back in a simple ponytail. Glasses perched on her small nose as she peered at the monitor.

"Hillary, this is Tessa Conway. I've told you about her; she works with me. Tessa, Hillary Basham."

Hillary looked up, vague surprise in her brown eyes. "Oh, yes, I remember. How are you?"

"Fine, thank you," Tessa said gently.

Sammy launched into a spirited explanation of his new computer, and Hillary was as carried away by it as he was. Tessa listened and nodded, trying to make sense of what they were telling her. They both seemed very excited, and because of that she asked questions, letting them enjoy the moment. Intuitively, she realized that Hillary was so much in love with Sammy that the girl was almost sick with it, but was too shy to let him know. Of course, with Sammy, a woman would have to put up a billboard and point it out to him to get him to notice it, and even then it might be a week before he realized he was the man involved. He was so deeply involved with his computer that everything else passed him by.

She didn't get her chess lesson that night; Sammy was so high from whatever great strides he'd made in the computer industry that there was no question of settling him down. He and Hillary played with the computer as if it were human, and they devoted over an hour to the naming of it before they finally settled on Nelda. Tessa groaned when she heard the name, and Sammy looked hurt, since it had been his idea. Hillary jumped in immediately in favor of Sammy's choice, and Nelda it was. Shaking her head, Tessa looked around at all of the equipment that Sammy had in his apartment. He must sink most of his salary into his hobby, she thought. In fact, she wondered how he even had money left to eat on.

Sammy wasn't a complete social wasteland; he eventually realized that he was hungry, and evidently recalled the manners his mother had tried for years to drill into him. Blushing, he jumped to his feet and offered to fix sandwiches and cold drinks, and refused Hillary's quick offer to help. He rushed out of the room and left a pool of silence behind him.

Tessa looked at Hillary's downcast eyes and saw the way the girl had suddenly withdrawn. "Where do you work?" she asked, since it was evident that Hillary wasn't going to begin the conversation.

"At a bank." Hillary gave her a shy look, then quickly looked down again. "Sammy talks about you a lot. You're...you're as beautiful as he says."

Tessa wondered if she'd gone too far in her friendship with Sammy, trying to make him more comfortable in female company. "That's sweet of him, but I'm not beautiful at all," she said honestly, and that brought up the bent blond head. "It's just that he's shy with women, and I talk to him and make him laugh. He talks about you a lot, too."

"Yeah, but that's different. I'm a buddy, someone to talk computers with." For a brief moment, hostility was plain in her brown eyes.

"Then talk about something else when you're with him." The last thing she wanted was to get involved in some sort of triangle, especially when the man in question couldn't see the forest for the trees.

"That's easy for you, but not everyone's a...a flirt like you!" As soon as she flared up, hot color rushed into Hillary's rather pale face and made it rosy. She looked down again, as if appalled at her rudeness, and Tessa sighed.

"Hillary, I'm not a threat to you. Please believe me. Sammy's just a friend to me, nothing else."

"But what about the way he feels about you?"

"He's definitely not in love with me; I promise!" Before she could say anything else to reassure the girl, Sammy came back into the room with a tray of drinks. He carefully set it down away from his equipment.

"I'll be right back with the sandwiches."

"I'll help!" Scrambling to her feet, Hillary hurried after him.

Feeling definitely *de trop,* Tessa called after them, "Just one sandwich for me; I have to be leaving soon."

When they came back into the room, Sammy frowned at her. "But we haven't played chess yet."

"It's later than I thought, and tomorrow is a working day," she reminded him.

He looked guilty. "I guess I got carried away over Nelda."

"I enjoyed hearing about Nelda," she reassured him.

"I know you've probably been bored, but really, I think we're going to be able to market Nelda. Hillary and I have put a lot of time and money into her; she's really something."

Was he talking about the computer or Hillary? Probably the computer. Deciding to give him a nudge in the right direction, Tessa said blandly, "It must be marvelous to have someone like Hillary, someone who understands your work and wants the same things you do."

Hillary flushed, but Sammy wasn't paying any attention. "Yeah, she's really great."

As quickly as she could without appearing rude, Tessa downed her sandwich and drank her cold drink, then gathered up her purse and light coat. "I really have to be going now."

Sammy walked her to the door. "I owe you a chess lesson," he said, smiling. "How about tomorrow night?"

For some reason, Tessa thought she'd probably had her last chess lesson. It was better not to cause trouble.

"I already have plans for tomorrow night, and I know you better than that, anyway! You're still going to be playing with Nelda to see if she can do everything you think she can."

He rubbed the back of his neck, shrugging his shoulders to work out the kinks. "You're probably right. We still have a lot of work to do on her. Maybe next week?"

"Maybe," she said, giving him a smile. He'd be so involved with his work that he'd never notice; she had been the one who had pursued their friendship, easing him out of part of his shyness.

Later that evening, when she was ready for bed, she sat with pillows behind her back and a pad of writing paper on her knees. Her weekly letter to Aunt Silver was its usual mixture of news and comment, and at the end of it she mentioned Brett Rutland. As she sealed the envelope she smiled to herself. She'd deliberately been casual in her mention of him, knowing that Aunt Silver's antennae would begin quivering as soon as she read the name.

Billie had brought coffee and doughnuts for their mid-morning break, and they had just begun their second doughnut when Tessa's phone rang. She answered it absently.

"I just want to confirm tonight. Six-thirty."

She hadn't heard his voice on the phone before, but there was no mistaking his identity. She closed her eyes briefly at the pleasure that rippled through her at just the sound of his voice. "Yes. Six-thirty."

"Do you like to dance?"

"Did granny wear garters?"

His low, rough laugh filled her ear. "Wear your dancing shoes."

When she hung up the phone, Tessa was aware that her heart wasn't beating in its regular rhythm, and she felt a little breathless. Even over the phone, his impact almost knocked her down. She thought of his thick, tawny brown hair and navy eyes, and it became even more difficult to breathe.

"Don't you ever stay at home?" Billie said automatically. It was practically standard procedure for Tessa to have at least one offer to go out every day.

"Of course I do. You know Monday night is laundry night."

They laughed together, but Tessa's mind was already on the coming night. They would have dinner, go out dancing...and then what? Would he try to make love to her again? She was afraid that he would, and even more afraid that he wouldn't.

Billie regarded her friend thoughtfully. "You know, this is the first time I've seen you get cloudy-eyed over a man. Is this one special to you?"

"I'm afraid he will be." Well aware of the admission in those few words, Tessa wound her suddenly shaking fingers together.

"You don't want to fall in love? Sometimes I think I'd give anything I own to find the right guy, the real McCoy." Why should Tessa, of all people, be nervous about a man? Of all the people Billie knew, Tessa was the most comfortable with men, a woman who honestly enjoyed a man's company. It didn't make sense for her to be so wary.

Tessa didn't volunteer Brett's name, and Billie didn't ask, for which Tessa was grateful. She didn't know how Brett felt about their connection being known, but she knew she wouldn't like the gossip that would flow as surely as the tides followed the moon if it became known that she was seeing Brett Rutland. His position automatically made their relationship difficult. She was totally uninterested in climbing the corporate ladder, but that wouldn't keep people from saying that she was trying to get ahead on the strength of her performance in the bedroom rather than in the office.

Because of her uneasiness at both the way she was beginning to feel about him and the difficult situation she could find herself in at work, she was quiet that night. She could feel his cool gaze dissecting her, trying to probe her thoughts. Over coffee, he asked, "Has something upset you?" His voice was so even that it took her a moment to hear the steel in it.

She blew across the steaming surface of the coffee, then sipped it. "Not really. I'm a little at a loss. Would you rather not have people from the office know we've been out together?"

"I don't give a damn who knows."

"I know I'm being premature in worrying about it. After all, we've only been out twice, and that doesn't mean—"

"Yes, it does mean," he interrupted, reaching for her hand. He put his hand on the table, palm up, and looked at her slender fingers as they lay across his palm. The contrast in their hands was striking, in ways besides the obvious one of size. His hands were powerful, lean and hard, with long fingers and short clean nails, his fingertips rough, his skin bronzed. Her hands were slim and delicate, the bones so fragile that her fingers were almost translucent, her oval nails polished. Her hands bore no rings.

"Have you ever been married?" he asked abruptly, looking at her bare fingers.

"No."

"Engaged?"

She sipped her coffee for a moment before replying. "Twice."

His eyes narrowed. "What happened?"

"I found out that I didn't love either of them enough."

"You must have thought you did, at one time."

She sighed and looked away from him. She didn't particularly want to talk about her failed engagements, which to her were almost as bad as failed marriages, but she could sense his determination to get the details out of her.

"The first time, it was an infatuation that I took for love, that's all. I was in college, and Will was a medical student. He wanted us to get married right away; he'd already planned for me to quit college and put him through school. I gave him his ring back."

He was watching her very closely, reading every nuance of expression that crossed her face. "And the second time?" he asked, dismissing Will as unimportant because he sensed her reluctance to continue.

"Andrew," she said slowly, somehow feeling compelled to answer him. "He did something that hurt me, and I didn't love him enough to forgive him."

After several moments of silence, Brett realized that she wasn't going to enlarge on her explanation. His hand tightened on hers. "Tell me," he insisted. The dim light above his head turned his tawny hair into dark gold and cast shadows on his face that made it seem harder, more dangerous.

Her hand moved restlessly in his. "I don't believe in raking over old coals. I don't think about it anymore. I picked up the pieces and moved on."

"Tell me," he whispered, his eyes as dark as midnight.

"He was unfaithful." Simple words, old-fashioned words, but for her they were the epitaph for a romance. With her heart, Tessa gave fidelity, and she expected the same in return. Andrew had cheated her, promising her faith and giving her only deceit.

Brett's eyes brushed over her throat and shoulders and breasts, his gaze as hot as a touch. "He was a fool. Why would any man want to sleep around when he could have you in his bed every night?"

Tessa looked up at him, and color rose in her cheeks at the way he was looking at her. Still holding her hand, he rose to his feet. "Dance with me," he invited.

She went willingly into his arms, grateful for the hard strength that enfolded her, for the warmth of his body. The virile impact of his masculine appeal made her tremble, but being in his arms also made her feel safe, as if his strength held the rest of the world at bay. She put her arms around his shoulders, sighing a little in contentment.

"Did you enjoy your chess lesson?" he murmured, brushing her soft hair and temple with his lips.

She laughed against his throat. "We never got around to it. Sammy was so excited over his new computer that he couldn't think about anything else."

"What sort of new computer?"

"Nelda. He swears it's going to revolutionize the personal computer industry, and maybe it will. For his sake, I hope so. He has to have a small fortune sunk into all of that equipment he has in his apartment. I don't see how he can afford to eat."

Above her head, Brett's eyes narrowed as he filed that bit of information away in his memory. Automatically his arms tightened about her, pulling her closer so that her breasts flattened against his muscled chest. "Did you tell him there wouldn't be any more chess lessons?"

"No, there was no need. He's so involved with Nelda, he won't even notice."

"Why did you get involved with him in the first place? He isn't your type."

Tessa stiffened a little in his arms. "He's a nice man; why isn't that my type?" She seldom bothered herself enough to take offense at anything anyone said, but she couldn't ignore Brett. She was vulnerable to him in ways she didn't even want to think about. Just what did he think her "type" was?

"He'll never be the life of the party," Brett said coolly. "And for all his electronic genius, you could wind him around your little finger and he'd never realize it. If you had him as steady company, you'd be bored to tears within a week."

She stared up at him, trying to read his thoughts in his hooded enigmatic eyes. She was more than a party-girl, and she wanted him to see that, to see the woman beneath the gay and frothy facade. Did he think she was just out for a good time, that she was only attracted to people who were as comfortable socially as she was? "I'm never bored with Sammy," she said, her voice steady, concealing the faint hurt that was welling in her. "I like him very much, whether he's my type or not."

Slowly his arm tightened about her waist, pulling her so close to him that his hard body felt imprinted against her softer one. "He doesn't matter, since you won't be seeing him again. I want you; I'm going to have you. And I don't share.''

Tessa caught a quick breath at the hard, determined note in his voice. She was accustomed to being pursued, but Brett was a man who not only chased, but caught his prey. Her frail butterfly wings would be useless against his power, yet she wouldn't feel threatened at all if she knew she could entrust herself to him. Did he want her for herself, or did he only want to conquer her because of the challenge she represented, to catch the fragile and elusive butterfly simply so he could say she'd belonged to him for a while?

Perhaps he saw some of her doubts reflected on her face, in her clear green eyes, because he slid his hand down to boldly cup her bottom, propelling her forward to press her hips against his in a gesture so provocative and possessive that she barely stifled the startled cry that came to her lips. ''Get used to it,'' he drawled, and something frightening moved in his navy eyes.

Her face burning, Tessa looked around hastily to see if anyone had seen him, but no one was paying any attention to them, and she felt her color begin to fade. The evening, which had begun so quietly, was getting out of hand. ''I want to go home now, please,'' she told him evenly.

''Are you certain? It's still early.''

''Yes, I'm certain. I'd like to go now.''

Perhaps she was being foolish in abandoning a public place for a private one, but Tessa felt that she could

handle herself better without an audience. He wasn't the
kind of man to force a woman; she had no fear that the
evening would end in a wrestling match. Even given the
provocation of the way she'd kissed him the first time
they'd gone out together, he'd been more understanding than she would have expected any man to be, under
the circumstances. The problem was that when he kissed
her, she didn't want him to stop. Ever. And there was a
sensual determination about him now that made her
pulse rate increase. If he pressed the issue, would she
give in? She was weak, because she wanted very much
to give in; she wanted to be in his bed and give herself
to him. The strong physical attraction she'd felt for him
from the beginning was rapidly intensifying. She was
beginning to love him, despite everything her common
sense was telling her. She knew that he was a walking
heartache, a man who had such a strong sensual appeal to women that he probably couldn't even remember the names of those who had shared their beds with
him.

She was silent on the drive to her apartment, and so
was he, though occasionally she could feel his intent
gaze on her. If only she could read his thoughts! But he
kept them well-hidden, and she had no idea what he
wanted from her beyond the obvious: physical gratifi-
cation. To really know him would be a lifetime occu-
pation, she thought. He kept himself too well guarded;
he was so cool, so controlled even in his passion. The
woman who broke that control would find herself with

a volcano on her hands, but Tessa shivered with excitement at the thought of being that woman.

Once again he preceded her into the apartment and checked all of the rooms before returning her key to her. She stood still, a little wary as he approached her, and a faint smile touched his chiseled mouth as he put his hand beneath her chin and tilted her face up to him. "You pretty little witch," he whispered, his warm breath caressing her face. "You tie a man in knots with your flirt-and-retreat games. You can keep on flirting, baby, but I'm going to put an end to those teasing retreats. Kiss me. I've been driving myself crazy for two days, thinking about your mouth and the way you taste." He brushed his lips over hers in a light, tantalizing caress. "Kiss me," he demanded again, then took the choice away from her by fastening his mouth on hers, hard, his tongue going deep and again giving her his heady taste. Her eyes closed on a hot swell of pleasure, and her hands clenched his shoulders.

They stood entwined, their mouths greedy and clinging, until Tessa felt light-headed from lack of air and pulled her mouth free; then she bent her head and rested it against his shoulder. The want, the need, that vibrated between them was staggering, and from the pressure of his body she knew that he was strongly aroused, yet he seemed to be waiting for a signal from her. She couldn't give it to him; the act of physical love was an act of commitment for her, and she wasn't certain enough of her feelings on the basis of two meetings to let him have that intimacy. Gently he rubbed the back of her neck, easing the tension in the taut tendons he found there.

"Let's go to bed," he murmured, kissing her temple and the shell of her ear, outlining the rim of her ear with the very tip of his tongue and setting off small ripples of pleasure that flowed over her body. "I know you think it's too soon, but waiting won't change anything. I'm going to have you, and we both know it."

She closed her eyes in an agony of wanting and indecision. He was so warm and strong, and she wanted him so much that she was nothing but an empty ache inside. "I'm afraid I'm going to fall in love with you," she blurted, her voice muffled against his shoulder, and she knew that she lied. She was afraid, yes, because it was far too late for her; she was already so much in love with him that she couldn't pull back now, and no lecture from her common sense was going to change it. She'd been waiting for him all of her life. She could no more halt the tide of her emotions than she could stop breathing.

Brett went very still. Even the hand on the nape of her neck ceased its motion. Love, in the romantic sense, wasn't something that existed for him, and it wasn't something that he wanted. Until she'd said the word, the idea hadn't even occurred to him. He'd taken her out to dinner the first time for a twofold reason: because he wanted to take her to bed, and to question her about the other employees at Carter Engineering. His physical desire had increased until the heat of it seared him, until he couldn't sleep and tossed restlessly on the twisted sheets, his body taut and frustrated. She intrigued him as no other woman had ever done; she was both bold and wary, inviting and resisting at the same time. For the first time in his life, he resented the thought of other men. He didn't want her associating with Sammy Wallace for a reason quite apart from the fact that the man was a suspected embezzler. He wanted all her time to be his, all her kisses to be his, and a primitive possessiveness ate at him. When he thought of the two men she'd been engaged to, he wanted to shake her for allowing them to get close enough to her that she'd even considered marriage.

But he didn't want the entanglements of emotion. Love was greedy and demanding, and he didn't want that sort of emotional intimacy. His mind was always a little aloof, always in control, and he wanted to stay that way; he'd seen too many men make complete fools out of themselves, all in the name of some confused emotional high that they called love.

Already Tessa was intruding into his thoughts, when he should have his mind strictly on business. The image of her sleek, silky body stretched out on white sheets, waiting for him, was one that burned in his mind at all hours, entering his thoughts when he least expected it. She was distracting him from the clandestine cat-and-mouse game he and Evan were playing with a thief, and he wanted to take her, satiate himself with her, so he could put her out of his thoughts and get on with the job at hand.

The thought of her falling in love with him jolted him. What would it be like to have this fancy, flirty woman belonging to him? Could she love, or was she just playing with the word? Had she really loved either of those men she'd been engaged to? What had she said about the one who had been cheating on her? That she didn't love him enough to forgive him? Perhaps it was all just a game to her, to lure a man deeper and deeper into the trap of her charm. But at the same time, the idea tantalized him, much like the subtle perfume she wore that drifted to his nose every so often, then faded elusively.

Tessa correctly read his stillness, and she fiercely blinked back the sudden scalding of tears, taking care to keep her head buried against his shoulder. "Why don't we call a halt to this now?" she whispered. "I don't know if I can keep it under control on my part, and I'd rather walk away from it before I get hurt." More lightly, she said, "We could always remember each other as the one that got away."

He put his hands on her shoulders and pushed her a little away from him so he could see her face, and a frown laced his brows. "No," he said curtly, not wanting to examine too closely his reason for rejecting her suggestion, but there was no way he was going to let her walk away from him. Her laughter would echo in his mind for the rest of his life, and he'd feel the ache of unsatisfied desire.

"Please." Her eyes were very clear and direct. "I told you, I don't sleep around. I don't have casual affairs. I have a lot to give a man; I'm more than just someone for fun and games, and I expect a lot from a man. If you aren't willing to give it, then let me go free."

"What do you expect from a man?" he asked roughly, drawing her closer to him once again, because he couldn't tolerate the distance between them.

"Friendship. Passion. Faith and trust and fidelity." She moved her head in a quick motion. "Love."

"I'm too old to believe in fairy tales, baby. Love is just a word that people throw around as an excuse for making fools of themselves." His hard hands hurt her shoulders. "I want you, and you want me. Let that be enough."

She shook her head again, but before she could say anything he bent his head and kissed her, slow and hard and deep, and again she was helpless against the black magic he practiced on her flesh. His hands moved over her body, touching her breasts and hips and thighs, as if branding her with his touch. When he pulled away, his face was full of dark color and his eyes were burning. "Think about that tonight. I'll pick you up tomorrow night at seven."

"There's no point in it," she said weakly, but she doubted that he heard her. He was already going out the door, and she stood there in the middle of the floor for a long time, her head bent, her eyes closed. He wasn't going to let her play it safe, and she wondered if she'd be able to survive another failed relationship.

She was torn between the instinctive need to protect herself and the needs of her deeply passionate heart, which told her to reach out and grab him, to twine herself about him so tightly that he'd never be able to get her out of his heart or mind. She had no chance at all if she was too cowardly to take one. Love gave, instead of demanded, and she wanted to give herself to him. Perhaps his mind didn't recognize love, but his body would. She was afraid...but it was too late for fear.

Evan rubbed his eyes tiredly, then returned to the stack of computer printout sheets before him. "I'm so tired, none of this is making any sense," he muttered.

Brett checked his watch; it was a little after midnight. He'd welcomed the intense concentration required by their investigation; it took his mind off his frustration, off his empty bed. But he was tired, too, and he had the nagging feeling that he'd been missing something, something that he'd have seen if he hadn't been so tired, if a part of his mind hadn't still been on Tessa. Damn her, why couldn't he stop thinking about her? She was just another woman, despite her laughing eyes and searing kisses. "We're missing something," he muttered. "Something is right here under our noses, and we're passing over it."

"A 747 could be under my nose right now and I'd have a hard time seeing it," Evan yawned, tossing his pencil down. "This guy has to be a real genius. Why don't you just offer him a bonus if he'll tell us how he's doing it?"

"You're pretty sure it's Wallace?" Brett asked, slanting Evan a quick, hard look.

"It's someone who knows how to play hardball with a computer, that's for sure."

"Tessa told me that he has a fortune in electronics in his apartment. He knows all the access codes; he can get into our computers any time he wants."

"I checked the guard's records, and he works late a lot of nights, but damn it, I can't find anything!" Evan said fiercely.

"It's here; we just haven't matched everything up yet." Brett got to his feet, moving restlessly around the hotel room. Damn, but he was getting tired of hotels, of living out of a suitcase. He wanted the crisp, clean air of the mountains, the wood-smoke smell of a roaring fireplace, the surging power of a horse beneath him. He moved his broad shoulders as if flexing against invisible chains, and the irritation of the job ate at him.

Evans rose, too, and stretched his tired muscles. "I'm calling it quits for the night. The weekend is ahead of us. I can do a lot more work then, when I don't have to spend the day pretending to study systems and options. I'm making a quick trip back to San Francisco in the morning, but I'll be back by Saturday morning at the latest. Do you need anything from the office?''

"No," Brett said absently, staring out the window at the sea of lights that stretched as far as he could see. Like New York, Los Angeles never slept. On the ranch, when night came, the livestock bedded down and so did the people.

After Evan had gone to his own room, Brett still stood at the window, but he no longer saw the lights. His body felt the pressure of her soft flesh against him, and his jaw tightened. He wanted her. He didn't even have to think her name; all other women became faceless, without identity, even sexless, when compared with her.

He gave the hotel bed a disgusted look, knowing that he wouldn't be able to sleep when he did finally lie down in it. His bed at the ranch was big and wide, and suddenly he pictured her in it, her soft dark hair spread across his pillow while she slept quietly, with the quilts pulled up over her bare shoulders to protect her from the frosty bite of the early spring morning. He shook his head to dislodge the picture, but it remained with him, and another disturbing image joined it: that of long winter nights, of making love to her in that bed, and knowing that the next night he'd have her again.

He scowled. He wasn't going to let her get to him like that. He'd take her and then forget about her, because in the taking he'd find that she was just like all the other women he'd had and then forgotten.

Chapter Four

Tessa was always at her desk a little early, and today Sammy brought in a cup of coffee for her before it was time to start work. "I couldn't remember if you took cream and sugar or not, so I brought both," he said, flushing a little as he dug in his pockets and produced two packets of sugar and a small plastic container of nondairy creamer, with a peel-off top.

She took the coffee gratefully; after lying awake half the night, she'd overslept a little and had missed her usual leisurely breakfast. She felt more than a little bruised, and only the assurance of her mirror had given her the courage to face the day. She looked normal, except for faint circles under her eyes, but she didn't feel normal. "You may have saved my life," she sighed. "Thanks, Sammy. I missed breakfast this morning."

He shifted his weight from one foot to the other. "We've been working on Nelda practically all night. Hillary's really great, isn't she? I don't have to explain things to her; she already knows."

"She's perfect for you," Tessa said firmly. It went right over his head.

"I'd still be putting Nelda together if Hillary hadn't been helping me. She has some contacts who might be able to help us with marketing Nelda, too; she meets all sorts in the bank."

"She's a wonderful girl. Very pretty, too."

He looked a little surprised. "Well, yeah, but the best thing about her is that she's so smart. She wrote the program for Nelda."

Tessa gave up; she'd done everything but propose to him for Hillary. She doubted that any woman held the same degree of fascination for him as Nelda did, but that was Hillary's problem. Right now, Tessa felt that she had a large problem of her own to worry about, and that problem was about six-four with indigo eyes. Hadn't she known from the start that Brett Rutland was more than she could handle?

She caught a movement just past Sammy's shoulder, and she looked up, feeling her heart skip a beat as she met Brett's narrowed eyes. He gave Sammy a hard look, then turned that look on her. "Good morning," he said, but Tessa heard the anger under the cool tones.

"Good morning," she returned evenly. "Mr. Rutland, this is Sammy Wallace, from data processing. Sammy, Brett Rutland."

Sammy thrust out his hand with a quick, awkward movement, and his face lit with eagerness. "Nice to meet you!"

With impeccable control, Brett shook hands. "I've heard a lot about you, Mr. Wallace. You're something of a genius with computers, aren't you?"

Sammy glowed. Before he could say anything, however, Perry Smitherman came rushing over, having spotted Brett. He practically skidded to a stop when he reached them. "Mr. Rutland!" Perry cried with a pleasure so obviously feigned that Tessa winced for him. "May I help you with something, sir?"

"Yes," Brett said curtly. "I'd like to speak with you privately, and I thought I'd stop by on my way up to the office. There's some information I'd like you to get for me."

"Yes, of course, of course," Perry babbled. "Right this way—my office—"

With a nod to both Tessa and Sammy, Brett went into Perry's office, with Perry skittering around him like a nervous poodle.

"Can you believe that?" Sammy asked incredulously. "He's actually *heard* of me." He was beaming with pleasure, his eyes sparkling behind the lenses of his glasses.

Tessa sat very still, but Sammy didn't notice her lack of response; he was too bemused and too pleased to notice anything. It was time for him to be on the job, so he ambled out as casually as he'd ambled in. Tessa turned on her video screen but sat staring at the blinking cursor without really seeing it. Brett had been as controlled as usual, but she was acutely sensitive to his mood, and she'd felt the seething anger beneath his calm exterior. Had something happened this morning to put him in a bad mood, or was he angry because he'd walked in and found her talking with Sammy? He'd expressly ordered her not to see Sammy after working hours, but this was on the job; surely he didn't expect her to go out of her way to avoid the people she worked with? It was ridiculous even to think that he might be jealous of Sammy. Sammy wasn't even in the same class with Brett, and Brett had to know it. She'd also told him that Sammy was just a friend, but he'd been glaring at Sammy as if he'd like to take a swing at him, and poor Sammy wouldn't even have an inkling of what was going on.

Was Brett jealous? The possibility made her almost dizzy with hope. He had no reason to be, but wouldn't jealousy signal that he cared more deeply for her than she'd thought?

Tessa was good enough at her job, and disciplined enough, that she managed to be productive even though she kept one eye on Perry's door, waiting for Brett to reappear. She was jittery and excited, and she smiled a little in amusement at herself, because none of her friends here would ever believe that Tessa Conway could be nervous over a man. The difference was that Brett wasn't just *a* man, he was *the* man, and that was quite a lot of difference. Not even Andrew had ever made her feel the way she felt with Brett, and at the time Tessa had thought herself sincerely in love with Andrew. She was learning that there were many different degrees of love, and that the deep, hungry need she felt for Brett far surpassed anything she'd even imagined.

At last Brett came out of Perry's office, but he passed her without even glancing in her direction. Tessa felt a pang of unreasonable hurt; after all, she'd been the one who'd said that she would feel uncomfortable with office gossip, so Brett was only following her wishes in not making their relationship obvious. But she found that she still wanted something from him: a look, a smile, anything to reassure her that he didn't feel as cold as he looked.

Whatever he'd wanted from Perry, evidently Perry hadn't found it to be a pleasant visit. Through the open door of Perry's office, Tessa could see him pacing back and forth, alternately wringing his hands or shoving his fingers through his thinning hair. She'd heard that Brett often had that effect on the executives and department heads who had to deal with him. There were two sides to his personality, and she felt a little disoriented because she couldn't quite reconcile the coldly scathing executive who tore strips of hide off anyone who crossed him with the man of burning sensuality who kissed her with such sweet fire.

How could she find herself so helplessly in love with a man she didn't really know? He was a puzzle to her, his personality an intricate maze that she longed to solve, because she felt that her reward for finding the secrets of his personality would be a fiery love that would last a lifetime.

By noon, the fact that Brett Rutland had had a private meeting with Perry was all over the office. "What's going on?" Billie asked eagerly over lunch. "Is Perry in trouble?"

"Not that I know of," Tessa said, startled at the thought.

"Then why did Rutland have a private meeting with him?"

"Now, you know you're always telling me not to get too friendly with people," Tessa said innocently. "What was I supposed to do, go up to the man and say, 'Mr. Rutland, honey, what are you doing in here?'"

"No one would be surprised," Billie grumbled. "And the hell of it is, he'd probably say, 'Miss Conway, honey, why don't I take you out to dinner tonight and tell you all about it?'"

Yes, he might say exactly that, Tessa thought, and smiled. She had to be a blue-ribbon fool, but she longed for the hours to pass so she could see him again, even knowing that he wasn't in the best of moods and that he was hard to handle even when he was feeling good. But she wanted to see him; she wanted to rest her head on his hard chest and soak up his nearness, like a flower soaking up the sun. She'd known him less than a week, but he'd embedded himself so deeply in her thoughts that it was difficult for her to remember how it had been before, when there had been no tall man with tawny hair and navy eyes who overshadowed every other man she'd ever known, who had taken over her dreams in daylight and dark. Was there a moment in her life now when she was actually unconscious of him? She couldn't think of one. Even when she was asleep, he was in her mind, so that she went to sleep thinking of him and woke to a continuation of the same thought, as if he had been there all along.

"You've gone moony-eyed again," Billie said, watching her. "Whoever he is, he must be something else."

Tessa caught her breath. "He is."

"It's Brett Rutland, isn't it? The way you smiled a moment ago, when we were talking about him...I can't describe it."

There was no use in denying it, since Tessa felt that she couldn't control her expression right then, and in any case she wasn't inclined to deny the way she felt about him. She wasn't ashamed of loving him; she felt glorified by it, as if she were more alive now than she'd ever been before in her life. "Yes," she admitted quietly.

Billie was concentrating fiercely. "Did you meet him for the first time this week, in the elevator?"

"Yes. We had dinner that night...and last night."

"You've been out with him twice, and you think you're in love with him? The Ax-Man? Tessa, there can't be two people any more mismatched than you and Brett Rutland! You're the life of any party, and he...well, picture it yourself. He walks into a room, and it's instant silence."

That was the public Brett; Billie would never comprehend the potent charm he could exert in private, the intense concentration he turned on a woman that demanded the same degree of attention in return. But Tessa had known his kisses, felt the heat of him straining against her, and she would never be able to think of him as the cold, ruthless troubleshooter who reported only to Joshua Carter.

"Will you keep this to yourself?" she asked Billie. "He said that he doesn't mind who knows, but I don't like the thought of everyone gossiping about us."

"Sure," Billie agreed readily, and reached over to pat her hand. "You didn't pick an easy one to fall for, did you?"

"Of course not." Tessa's soft mouth curved wryly. "The easy ones were all too...easy."

Billie felt that she'd been watching out for Tessa ever since the younger woman had moved to Los Angeles, but never before had she felt that Tessa was heading for deep trouble. Even when she'd just begun to adjust to the differences between Tennessee and California, Tessa had always approached everything with high spirits and good humor. But Brett Rutland could break Tessa's bright spirit with his cool ruthlessness if Tessa cared too much and he cared too little. Billie's eyes were troubled as she looked at her friend. "If you need me, all you have to do is pick up the telephone and call me," she offered. "I can always offer you a drink, an extra bed and a shoulder to cry on, singly or in any combination."

"Thanks. I know that you're there for me if I need you." Tessa smiled warmly at her friend. "But don't be so glum! I've always landed on my feet before, haven't I?"

"You haven't been in love before," Billie retorted. "Believe me, love can be hell."

Yes, it could be, and Tessa had already been singed by its fires, but the small flames Andrew had generated were nothing compared to the inferno Brett lit just by walking into the room. Faintly confused, because she'd never before doubted that she'd loved Andrew, she was now beginning to wonder if she'd ever been more than fond of him. There was simply no comparison between the way she'd felt then and the way she felt now about Brett. With Brett, she felt an irresistible compulsion to walk into his arms and never leave them, to simply press herself against him and cling until her flesh had melded with his, until they were no longer two separate beings but a part of each other, eternally linked in flesh and heart and mind. When she wasn't with Brett, she felt...lonely, and she'd never been lonely before in her life. She'd been alone many times, and enjoyed her solitude as much as she enjoyed the company of friends, but now she felt oddly incomplete.

When Brett came to her apartment that night, Tessa had only to look at him to know that he was angry. His anger wasn't violent, but it was all the more potent for his control. Her spine felt chilled as she looked up into his narrowed eyes. "If you don't want to break off with Wallace, all you have to do is say so. I don't like being lied to."

"I haven't lied to you," she replied steadily. "Sammy is a friend, nothing more. We work on the same floor; I'm forever running into him. I can't hide under my desk to keep from seeing him."

There was something primitive in his expression as he looked down at her, and he touched her delicate jaw with hard, lean fingers, a light touch that nevertheless shocked her with its possessiveness. "Don't ever lie to me," he rasped; then he bent down and kissed her.

It seemed as if it had been forever since she'd tasted him, felt his mouth move hungrily on hers, and she raised her hands to his shoulders to cling to him. Shaking slightly, reveling in the delight that crashed through her in response to his lightest touch, she kissed him with all the sweet fire she could give him. Finally, he raised his head, his eyes searing, and a faint film of perspiration had broken out on his forehead.

The tension between them increased as the night grew older. Though she loved seafood, Tessa could do little more than pick at her lobster, because every nerve ending in her body was picking up the signals of his sensual arousal, and a hot, answering need coiled achingly inside her. He made her feel so female that it was as if she'd never before had any concept of her own femininity. With him, she was a primitive, and the intensity of her emotions frightened her, but at the same time she was lured by their power. The time for running away was past; perhaps it had been too late for her from the first moment she'd looked up into the blue beauty of his eyes.

"Spend the day with me tomorrow," he said abruptly, for the first time in his life putting his personal concerns ahead of business. There was a job to be done, but it paled in importance when compared to the urgency he felt to consolidate his relationship with Tessa. When he'd seen Sammy Wallace hovering over her desk that morning, he'd been seized by a cold rage that had made him want to choke the man. He'd never been possessive of a woman before, but women had come to him so easily and so early that he hadn't valued them for anything other than physical pleasure. But Tessa hadn't offered herself to him; she'd enticed him with her teasing smile and laughing eyes, then danced away from his touch. He was a man, and a hunter. He'd have her, and soon.

"Yes," Tessa agreed, though it hadn't been an invitation as much as a command. Her eyes wandered over his hard, rough face, and a tightness in her chest warned her that she'd forgotten to breathe again.

He swore softly, the words a barely audible rasp. There was a soft, drowning look on her face that made his body tighten in need. "Let's get out of here," he rasped, surging to his feet and pulling her from her chair. She didn't protest; she was silent as he paid the bill; then she leaned on him a little on their way out to the car.

The night had turned cool, and Tessa lifted her flushed face to the fresh breeze. She felt heated, as if her internal furnace were burning away at top capacity, and she wanted to remove the clothing that was suddenly too restrictive. He unlocked the car door and opened it, then put her inside, and Tessa drew a deep, shuddering breath. How could she control the wild need inside her? It was burning her up, turning her body into a cauldron of love and wanting. When he got behind the steering wheel, she said, "Brett," in a dazed voice, and reached out for him.

He jerked as her hands touched his chest. "You're driving me out of control," he said in a low, savage tone. "I want to push you down on the car seat and take you right now. Damn it, if that's not what you want, too, then don't tease me now, because you're skating on thin ice."

She was barely in control herself, but she heard the taut warning in his voice, and she moved away from him, clenching her hands in her lap in an effort to resist the need to touch him. Did he really think she was only teasing him? The party girl wasn't laughing now; she loved, and she wanted, and she hurt. Why was love portrayed as the ultimate happiness when it was so painful? Her emotions for him were so powerful and deep that she felt as if the greater part of herself, the essence of her very being, had been taken away from her own control and placed in his hands. Love like that was a sword, and in loving Brett she was balanced precariously on the cutting edge; he wasn't a safe man to love. She risked more than her heart in loving him; she risked her very life, for that was what he meant to her, and if anything happened to him the light would go out of her life, and her laughter would fade away. It was frightening to love anyone like that, but Tessa found that, with Brett, her protective barriers of wit and laughter were useless. He demolished them with his intense masculinity and tapped the deep vein of passion within her. She had always thought herself capable of loving deeply, but until Brett, she hadn't known just how deeply.

He drove a little too fast, and when she glanced at him she saw that his jaw was set, and his sensual mouth was pressed into a grim line. He looked hard and dangerous, not the sort of man a woman should play with. In more primitive times, he would probably have thrown her over his shoulder and carried her off. Tessa glanced at him again, and a shiver ran down her spine, because there was a ruthlessness in his face that frightened her a little.

When they reached her apartment, he silently took the key from her and opened the door, then stepped back for her to enter. Tessa switched on the light and turned to face him, but whatever she'd meant to say was forever lost as he closed the door and locked it. She caught her breath, her eyes lifting to his. His eyelids had drooped sensually, so that only a thin line of navy blue was revealed, but his intent was plain to read. Without a word, he shrugged out of his coat and unknotted his tie, pulling it free from his collar, then tossed the discarded garments over the back of a chair. "Now," he whispered harshly, his eyes never leaving hers, "come here and touch me."

Blindly, Tessa walked into his arms.

His mouth was hungry and hurtful, but her mouth clung to his in a trembling ecstasy that asked for all he could give her. Her ribs were crushed by the almost brutal grip of his arms, but she couldn't get close enough to him. She ached at the hateful separation of their flesh. She heard husky little whimpers, but though she didn't recognize them as her own, Brett heard them, and everything male in him responded to those feminine sounds of pleasure. He bent her over his arm, and his mouth left hers to sear a path down the smooth column of her throat, down even more to the firm jut of her breasts. He fastened his mouth on her flesh, and even through the fabric of her dress she felt his moist heat, and desire so sharp that it was painful sliced through her.

She sagged abruptly against him as her knees wobbled and lost their ability to hold her upright. Just as swiftly, he swung her up in his arms and took the few steps to the closest chair, settling into it with her draped over his lap. Tessa opened her love-drugged eyes, the green depths deep and dreamy as she looked at him. Her hands wound around his strong neck. "I've tried not to love you," she whispered achingly, unable to hold her love secret, "but I can't stop myself."

A strong shudder rolled through him at her words. It didn't matter how many other men had heard the words of love from her luscious mouth. It didn't even matter that he'd never wanted a woman to love him. He'd always been coolly indifferent to any feelings of devotion he might have aroused...until Tessa. She was a challenge like none he'd encountered before. It wasn't the resistance she'd put up against him, because she really hadn't resisted him at all. Rather, she'd eluded him, letting him glimpse her womanly richness, then flitting away out of reach. She was so intensely female that he instinctively wanted her; she was a woman who could match the fierceness of his masculinity. In loving him, she gave herself to him, and he wasn't inclined to let her go free again.

His left arm under her back, he arched her up to meet the hungry possession of his mouth, while with his free hand he began opening the line of tiny buttons that marched down the front of her dress. Tessa trembled in his grasp, but didn't protest. She didn't want him to stop; she wanted him to love her like this forever. She'd learned that there was a time for giving and a time for taking. This was her time to give. She'd give all of herself to the man she loved, freely, with all the loving generosity of her nature. Her heart was slamming against her rib cage so violently that she felt dizzy, and in an effort to get more air she turned her head away from his kiss, exposing the tender, elegant line of her throat to him. He explored it with his hot mouth, and Tessa made a little whimpering sound. She wanted him; she needed him so much that she ached deep inside, and she clutched at him with desperate fingers.

"Slow down, slow down," he murmured, easing the dress off her shoulders. "I want this to last a long time. Let's get this off you, so I can see you; I want to strip you naked and touch you all over."

She pulled her arms out of the sleeves and lay back into the cradle of his arm, letting him look his fill at the way her breasts pushed at the thin silky fabric of the white camisole she wore. She hadn't worn a bra, so the dark pink nubs of her hardened nipples were clearly outlined, the small tips begging for his attention. His breath came harder and faster as he lifted her up and tugged the dress down around her hips, then pushed it down her legs and off. She lay on his lap, and his eyes burned her flesh as they moved slowly over her body. Besides the camisole, her only garments were her matching tap pants, a delicate lace garter belt, silk hosiery and her fragile high-heeled sandals. His hand drifted over her body, learning the contours of her, stroking her silk-clad legs until he reached her ankles. Slowly he removed her shoes and let them drop; then his fingers trailed back up her legs. He fingered the elastic of her garters, and a look of almost brutal desire hardened his face.

"You should be put under lock and key," he said gutturally, never taking his eyes from the path his hand traveled. His fingers curled under the waistband of her tap pants and he pulled them down, revealing the soft little hollow of her navel. He circled it with a gentle finger, then the as-yet uncovered riches of her body lured him on, and his hand moved upward to her breasts. He fondled her, his hand burning her flesh. Tessa twisted on his lap, wanting him to push the camisole away and touch her bare flesh.

"Please," she begged softly, arching up to him.

"What is it you want?" he whispered. "Is it this?" He slid his hand inside the camisole and cupped her breast, his thumb rasping over her taut nipple and setting it on fire.

Tessa moaned, squirming against him. "Yes. Yes." She began trembling so violently that her entire body quaked, and he soothed her, cuddling her closer against his hard frame while his hand continued to stroke her breasts.

"Easy, honey," he crooned. "I'm going to give you what you want. Touch me; tell me what you want me to do to you."

The first part of his instructions was easy to carry out. Her hands were drawn to him anyway, and she put them on his chest, feeling the heat of his body burning through his shirt. But the second part.... How could she tell him, when all she knew was that she wanted him so badly she was dying from the exquisite pain of it? She was surrounded by his power, his sexuality.

"I don't know," she whispered shakily, clinging to him. She drew a deep, wavering breath. "I don't know how to handle you."

His blue eyes were so dark that they were almost black. "Sweetheart, you know exactly how to handle me. You know what I want."

"But that's the problem, I don't." Summoning up all her courage. Tessa gave him a tender, shaky smile. "Or rather, I know what you want, but I don't know how to go about it."

Brett went very still, his eyes burning as they searched hers. He considered the meaning of her words, and because he was so sensually aroused and acutely aware of her every reaction, he went straight to the heart of the matter. "Tessa, haven't you ever had a man before?"

"No." Her hands moved over his face. "I love you, and I want you to be the first."

A curious spasm crossed his face; then he surged to his feet, with her held high in his arms. "I'll show you," he muttered hoarsely. "I'll take care of you, honey. You don't have to be afraid."

He strode swiftly to her bedroom and shouldered the door open, then crossed the room and placed her on the bed. He turned on the bedside lamp, and she stared up at his hard face. He didn't look cool and aloof now. He was burning with desire, all other thoughts wiped out of his mind. Gently he removed the rest of her clothing, leaving her lying nude on her bed, and she made an instinctive move to shield her body from his probing gaze. "No, let me see you," he said, and held her arms above her head while he touched every inch of her with his eyes. Incredible that this lovely, delicate piece of femininity had never lain uncovered before a man's hungry eyes before. Incredible that no other man before him had sheathed himself in her sweet depths. Incredible, but he didn't doubt her for a moment. Her innocence was part of her elusiveness. Her lack of sensual knowledge had enabled her to call a halt to his lovemaking when a more experienced woman, knowing what pleasure was in store for her, would have succumbed to the temptation.

And she was his, his alone. A primordial instinct that he'd never before realized he possessed made him want to brand her as his, so no other man would ever think of trespassing. He straightened and began removing his clothing.

Tessa watched him, her mouth going dry with excitement, her eyes hungry as she watched every stage of his disrobing. She hadn't realized quite how muscular he was. When his shirt was tossed aside, she gaped at the ripple of muscles beneath his smooth, tanned skin. His chest was broad and hard, roped with muscles, and tightly curled dark hair spread across it. His abdomen was flat and hard, and his legs were the powerfully muscled legs of a horseman. He lay down on the bed with her and leaned over her, gathering her close to him, and Tessa's eyes widened as she was overshadowed by the sheer size of him. Being naked in bed with him made her realize acutely the difference in their size and strength. She was helpless against his strength. If she had any control at all in this situation, it was only because he allowed her to have it.

Her eyes filled with the instinctive fear every woman feels when lying down with a man for the first time. Brett saw it, and tenderness filled him. He leaned over her and began kissing her lightly, sweet kisses that didn't reveal the violence of his passion. No matter what it cost him, he wouldn't brutalize her. There would be time later for more urgent possessions, but not this time, not her first time. Still kissing her, he slowly began acquainting her with his touch.

Before long, Tessa was twisting in his arms again, her body on fire from the slow caresses that burned her flesh. He knew all her sweet places, and all of them felt the sorcery of his expert fingers. She dug her nails into his shoulders, her mind clouded with heat. She couldn't think; she couldn't do anything but arch and squirm, trying to find more of the maddening pleasure he was giving her. His hand was between her legs, and he was doing things to her that made tension coil unbearably deep inside of her. Tighter and tighter the coil became, and she sobbed at the unbearably delicious sensation that she was about to explode.

Brett rose above her, and settled himself intimately between her thighs. Catching her hips in his powerful hands, he held her still, and broached her virginity with excruciating slowness.

Tessa cried out as she felt herself being filled, but she wasn't aware that she'd made a sound. She was in the grip of something far more powerful than pain, something that banished everything from her consciousness except her body and the wildness that was crashing through her as he took her. This wasn't a simple, basic physical act. It was an act of possession, the forging of a link between them that wove the very fabric of their beings together. She gave and he took, but in the taking found that the complexion of everything had changed. With every slow thrust he branded her as his, yet the threads that bound her to him also bound him to her. Shuddering with the intensity of his pleasure, every inch of him scalded by her hot sweetness, he paused to gather his slipping control.

Her face in the lamplight was both agonized and exalted, her eyes closed as her breath rushed in and out in a broken rhythm. Something tightened in his chest at the sight of her. "Am I hurting you, love?" he murmured urgently, unaware of the word he'd used for the first time in his life.

"No," she moaned, her body undulating against him. "Yes...I don't know. Brett, I don't think I can stand this....I'm flying apart...."

"Shhh, it's all right," he soothed, beginning again the slow movements that set him on fire. "Let go, baby. I'll catch you; I'll take care of you. Come on, darling, come on." He moved against her, his teeth grinding as he strained to hold himself back, all of his attention focused on her, reading every response she gave him. His nude body gleamed with sweat, and his tawny hair was wet and dark.

Tessa's head rolled back and forth, and she cried out blindly. No words had been invented to describe the great waves of feeling that suddenly began crashing through her insides, making her surge upward. She cried his name. Then no other words were possible, nothing was possible except that she give herself completely to the impossible sensations he'd aroused with his powerful masculinity. Dimly she was aware of the way he was moving now, with urgent power, and she heard his deep, growling cries of completion.

In the quiet aftermath, they lay together in silent exhaustion, his face turned into her throat. Tessa smoothed his hair, gently stroked his back and shoulders, though she was so tired that she felt herself drifting to sleep as she lay there. But before she slept, there was something she had to tell him. "I love you," she murmured drowsily, a gift of words that came from her heart without premeditation. "Brett...love." The two words were synonymous to her. She was immediately asleep, like a child, lying trustingly in his arms.

Chapter Five

Sleep didn't come so easily for Brett; he shifted his weight away from her, knowing that she was far too delicate to bear his weight on her all night, although he'd have liked nothing better than to have remained where he was. She murmured an inaudible protest, and he eased her into his arms, soothing her with his touch. Her head found his shoulder as naturally as if they'd been sleeping together for years, and she nuzzled against him in her sleep, her silky dark hair spread across his shoulder and arm.

His clear-cut lips were pressed into a thin line as he replayed their lovemaking in his mind. She'd been all he'd expected, and more. No other woman in his life had driven him to such a frenzy of desire, and the fact that she'd been virgin had made it even more special, different in a way that he didn't know how to handle. He wasn't a man to leave anything to chance. When she'd told him that it was her first time, he'd realized that she wouldn't be prepared to protect herself from pregnancy, and he'd taken care of it. He didn't think that she'd even noticed when he'd paused for a moment. But when he'd been making love to her, buried deep inside her, he'd thought of what it would be like if he hadn't taken any precautions, and abruptly he wanted to make her pregnant; he wanted her to bear his child. He'd violently resented the need to be careful. He wanted to give her the essence of his manhood, the joining of their bodies in a miracle that became a baby, his baby.

He'd never before wanted to take a woman to the ranch, but he could see Tessa there as easily as if she'd been there all her life. She'd like the sturdy ranch house with its big fireplace, the vast expanses, the soaring mountains. He could see her riding beside him, her delicate, exotic face flushed with pleasure. And he could see her in his bed.

He smiled faintly. There was no doubt how his father would take to her. Was there a man on earth whom Tessa couldn't charm out of his socks? Given the fact that Tom frankly admitted to a decided weakness for women, Brett knew that he and Tessa would hit it off from the first. She'd have Tom wrapped around her little finger the minute he heard that lazy drawl of hers.

A memory pierced him, and he closed his eyes on a sharp pang of desire. "I love you," she'd said, the words soft and liquid, and he'd never known that they could sound so right.

The things he was thinking and feeling were totally foreign to him, and on some edge of his consciousness he bitterly resented Tessa for making him think them. Why couldn't she be like all the other women he'd taken? Just a good time in bed, a casual good-bye kiss, then he'd walk out of her life as free as he'd been when he'd walked in. That was what he'd expected, but it hadn't worked out like that. She'd given him what he wanted, the use of her sweet, soft body, but somehow in the giving she'd taken things from him that he hadn't wanted to offer.

Finally he shifted, stretching out his arm to snap off the lamp, and sudden darkness closed around him, but still he couldn't sleep. Her warm body against his side felt so good that he wanted to turn and press himself fully against her. Her breathing was barely perceptible, but he felt it fan against his skin. He'd slept with a lot of women, but he hadn't liked sleeping entwined; yet now he didn't want to let her go. A man could get used to this in a hurry.

He'd marry her, he thought coolly. She suited him, more than he'd thought possible. And once they were married, he'd put a final stop to the way she had of flirting with every man in the vicinity. She was his, and he wasn't going to stand by and watch her turn a man on with those slow smiles and that magnolia-and-honey drawl of hers.

A sense of satisfaction came over him as he imagined being married to her. Yes, that was exactly what he wanted. Marriage had never figured in his plans for the future, but Tessa had changed all that. The dissatisfaction he'd been feeling with his present life suddenly crystalized, and he knew what he was going to do. He'd marry Tessa, quit his job with Carter-Marshall and take her to Wyoming. Ranch life was what he wanted, what he liked best, and she'd fit right in. It was time old Tom was a grandfather, anyway. His first thought was of the sons he'd have with Tessa, then his imagination supplied the picture of a baby girl with Tessa's enchanting smile and wide green eyes, and a tumble of dark curls on her head. He broke out in a sweat. Hell, what was he letting himself in for? A daughter of Tessa's would keep him on pins and needles for years, wondering what wild young buck was sniffing around his baby girl, and his baby girl would probably be flirting like mad and encouraging those wild young bucks.

In the dark, an unwilling grin spread over his hard face. Life with Tessa would never be boring. And she'd said that she loved him. She'd marry him without question, whenever he wanted. All in all, it was a very satisfactory plan. He relaxed, hugging Tessa closer to him, her bewitching fragrance tantalizing him as he drifted into sleep.

Tessa woke first the next morning, made restless by the unfamiliar weight and warmth in her bed. When she opened her eyes, she found herself staring at the back of his head. During the night he'd turned over on his stomach and he was sprawled out on the bed, taking up his share of the bed and half of hers. Her breath caught at the sight of his tousled tawny hair, like a shaggy lion's, and her heart actually skipped a beat. Love so powerful that it hurt welled up in her, and she'd reached out a trembling hand to touch him before she realized what she was doing and drew it back. Let him sleep. What should she say to him this morning, anyway? How should she act? Surprised, she realized that she was nervous about facing him the morning after. The compulsive passion they'd shared had made them intimate physically, but she was unsure of where she stood in every other way.

Gingerly, she slid off the bed and grabbed up her robe, quietly leaving the room to take a shower. Her eyes were troubled. She'd told him how she felt about him, but not even in the most passionate moments between them had he indicated that he felt anything for her other than sexual attraction. That was powerful enough, she admitted wryly, standing under the shower head and letting the water hit her full in the face. Her body was tender and achy, reminding her of his strength, reminding her of what had happened between them the night before.

She paused, her thoughts drifting. It had been good, so good that she'd thought she would die from the sharp pleasure of it. So that was what it was like.... She'd never imagined it would be so wanton, and so exalted. So that was what it was like to give herself to the man she loved.

When she finished with her shower, she wrapped herself in the robe and peeked into her bedroom, but Brett was still asleep. She went into the kitchen and put on a pot of coffee and sat down at the table, folding her hands on the tabletop and staring at nothing, her thoughts absorbed by the man in her bed and the lovemaking they'd shared during the night. Despite his passion, she sensed that there was a part of him that remained aloof, untouched, some inner core that watched but didn't become involved. Why did he want so much from her, when he refused to share that part of himself? She didn't want to hold in her emotions; Tessa was too warmly responsive to constantly rein herself in. She wanted to give him everything that she could, but because of his reserve, she felt wary and uncertain of herself. She didn't like the feeling. She'd never been the sort of person to be uncertain. She was generally decisive, knowing immediately what she wanted, though she was equally realistic in estimating her chances of getting it.

She wanted Brett, wanted him with a fierce female need that she'd never before experienced. He'd become as necessary to her as the air she breathed.

The coffee finished brewing, and as she was pouring herself a cup she heard Brett stirring. Immediately she felt warm all over, and she felt her face flush. Taking a hasty sip of coffee, she burned her tongue, and her hands trembled. She set the cup down before she spilled the coffee all over herself. Stop acting like a teenager! she scolded herself, but not all the scolding in the world could calm her racing heart.

"Tessa."

His early morning voice was a raspy grumble, and a shiver of response raced down her spine. Slowly she turned her head and looked at him standing in her kitchen doorway wearing only a pair of dark blue briefs. Fascinated by his hard, tough masculinity, her eyes drifted down his body, examining him from head to toe, and not missing an inch in between. Heat began to color her face, caused by a mixture of excitement and embarrassment.

He'd been watching her expressive face, seeing the open admiration in the way she looked at him, and her bold innocence made him want to pick her up and take her back to bed. Then, incredibly, she blushed.

He crossed the floor to her, putting his arms around her and easing her against his chest. "Why the blushes?" he asked gently.

"Last night...I acted so...and the things I said..."

"And the things we did," he finished, smiling a little above her head. "Are you all right?" As much as he wanted to make love to her again, he'd felt the delicacy of her body with its slender, aristocratic bones, and he didn't want to hurt her.

"Yes," she sighed, leaning her head against him. Her hands slid around his taut waist, then began to search over the heavy muscles of his back. "A little achy, that's all."

He kissed the tumble of curls on her forehead, then brushed them back, schooling himself to patience. He could wait; not easily, but he could wait. Remembering his plans of the night before, he felt a sudden urge to begin putting them in motion. The sooner he could have her installed at the ranch, the better. "Next weekend," he murmured, "if I can manage to get free, I'll take you to the ranch."

Her head lifted from his chest, and her eyes sparkled with excitement. "The ranch! I'd like that. But why shouldn't you be able to get free? Even executives usually get an occasional weekend off."

"Usually," he agreed, smiling at her impatience. "But this isn't the usual job—" He broke off, frowning at himself. It wasn't like him to confide in anyone, especially about sensitive matters, but he'd nearly blurted the whole thing out to her. It was one more measure of how close she'd gotten to him, how deeply she'd embedded herself in his thoughts.

Attuned to him as she was, Tessa felt his abrupt tension. Her smile faded. "Brett? Is something wrong here?" Alert now, she remembered snatches of gossip about Brett Rutland. His appearance usually meant trouble, not for him, but for the people who had to deal with him. He was called the Ax-Man. He found the root of any trouble, and the people causing it were fired. And after talking with Brett the day before, Perry Smitherman had been a basket case. "Perry...is something going on in the bookkeeping department? Is it Perry?"

Instinctively he moved to cover his slip, though he was uneasy at how swiftly she'd picked up the correct thread. "No, nothing like that," he murmured, distracting her by bending down to kiss her. He held her mouth under his, leisurely tasting her, until the growing tightness of his body warned him to slow things down.

The ploy had worked, almost too well. She was clinging to his shoulders, her soft body pliant against him. He could have her now, he realized, and groaned aloud. The temptation was too great. Despite his concern for her, despite the fact that he needed to check in with Evan, he wrapped his arms around her and lifted her off her feet. Instantly her slender arms wound about his neck, and she began kissing him fiercely as he walked back to the bedroom with her dangling from around his neck.

Evan tried Brett's hotel room again, and again there was no answer. Frowning, he dropped the receiver back into its cradle. It wasn't like Brett to disappear when there was work to be done, or not to let someone know where to reach him. Brett was a hard man to know, but when it came to work, he was utterly dependable. This was the first time in Evan's memory that Brett Rutland hadn't been there when his job called for him.

Well, there was no point in worrying about it. Brett could take care of himself, and there was work to be done. Evan began going over the computer printouts again, straining his eyes at the difficult print. The ribbon on the printer needed replacing, too, which made his job that much more difficult. He still had that nagging feeling that he was missing something, something so obvious that he should have seen it from the beginning. One of these accounts was bogus; it had to be. But he'd spent hours tracking the accounts down, and so far every one of them was legitimate; he'd been systematically checking them off his list. It should be getting easier, like the last pieces of a jigsaw puzzle, but it wasn't working that way. Nothing seemed wrong, yet he couldn't shake the feeling that something was, if he could only see it.

Damn! The print swam before his eyes, and he squinted to refocus his gaze. He was going to go blind before this was over.

The phone at his elbow rang, and he snatched it up. "Evan Brady."

"Found anything yet?" Brett's raspy voice growled in his ear.

"Nothing. I was beginning to think someone had taken out a contract on you. I've been trying to get you all day."

"Nothing like that. I'm in my room now; I'll be there in a minute, as soon as I take a shower. Is there any coffee ready?"

Evan reached over and lifted the pot that he'd had brought up some time ago. Nothing sloshed. "I'll call room service."

Brett hurried through his shower, well aware that he'd spent the day making love instead of working as he should have been doing, but he just hadn't been able to walk away from Tessa. She was wildfire, burning through his veins, out of control. The way she responded to him drove everything else out of his mind, until nothing else mattered but having her again, fusing their bodies as tightly as he could, wiping out the separateness of their beings. When he'd left she'd been asleep, curled on her side in exhaustion. He'd straightened the tangled sheets and pulled the covers up over her bare shoulders, fighting the urge to get undressed again and crawl into bed beside her. She was the most powerful distraction he'd ever seen, but he had work to do, even if he was a little late in remembering it.

After putting on khaki pants and a blue pullover knit shirt, he went to Evan's hotel room and rapped on the door with his knuckles.

"It's open; come on in!"

Evan didn't look as tired as he had before, but he was irritable, and the overflowing ashtray on the table was a measure of his tension. The room was filled with stale blue smoke. He didn't question Brett about his extended absence. Evan had worked with Brett long enough to know how far Brett would let anyone probe into his life, and those boundaries didn't stretch very far.

Still, there was something about Brett, and Evan eyed him closely. He looked tired, and he needed to shave, but he looked...almost happy. Strangely satisfied. It wasn't easy to read Brett; he wasn't beaming, but there was a hint of contentment in his eyes, a small relaxation of the line of his mouth. A woman! Evan thought, and had to control a grin. And not just any woman, either. Tessa Conway. It had been a long time coming, and Evan had long ago decided that the woman didn't exist who could get under Brett's skin, but that was before he, and Brett, had met Tessa Conway.

Yawning, Evan got to his feet and stretched his cramped muscles. "I'm going to move around for a while before I become rooted to the chair."

Brett took his place and lifted the sheaf of printouts onto his lap, then stretched his long legs out and propped them on the coffee table in front of him. By the time room service delivered the pot of fresh coffee, Brett was frowning in concentration, everything else wiped out of his mind as he went over the printouts line by line, checking them with a pencil. Evan poured two cups of coffee and set one beside Brett, but he remained on his feet, prowling about the room.

"Stir crazy?" Brett muttered, checking yet another line.

"Yeah. And half-blind, too. The first thing I'm going to do Monday morning is see that that printer has a new ribbon in it."

The print was bad, Brett admitted. Two hours later, he felt as if his eyes were crossing, and he stopped, leaning his head back and pinching his nose at the point between his eyes. "Is the coffee gone?"

"We emptied it about an hour ago."

Brett checked his watch. It was almost midnight, and he wondered if Tessa was still asleep, or if she was restless without him. He wanted to work himself into exhaustion, knowing that he'd toss and turn if he didn't, thinking about her, wanting her again. Sleeping with her the night before had been oddly satisfying, as if holding her in his arms while they slept completed him in some way.

Looking back at the printout sheets, his eyes fell on a name that had recurred frequently in the payout sheets. What caught his attention was that the name was the same as Tessa's. "What's this Conway, Inc. that so many checks are made out to? What sort of business is it?"

"Supplier," Evan said. "They've been supplying Carter Engineering for years. Basic building materials. I checked it out."

Several minutes later, Brett looked up. "What about Conmay?"

"Weren't you listening? They're a supplier—"

"No, not Conway. Conmay," he said, stressing the last syllable.

"That's what I thought you said." Evan went very still, staring at Brett. "Conmay belongs to two men, Connors and Mayfield."

Brett's eyes were narrowed. "We have checks sent out to both a Conway, Inc., and a Conmay, Inc. Are they both legitimate?"

"I'll be damned if I know," Evan growled, crossing to Brett's side to lean down and squint at the two very similar names. "That slipped by me completely. I thought it was the same account."

Brett began flipping back through the pages they'd already checked, looking for the first entry for Conway, Inc. Instinct told him that they were on the right track. Conway, Inc.... If it hadn't been for the similarity to Tessa's name, he wouldn't have noticed it.

"We need a computer terminal," he said decisively, getting to his feet. "We might as well go to the source." It would be a lot easier to track down that account with access to the central computer.

"Might as well," Even agreed. Like Brett, he sensed success, and that banished his fatigue. They could work as long as they liked, without fear of detection, for it was Saturday night, almost Sunday morning, and the building would be deserted except for the guards.

By three o'clock Sunday morning, they were both certain that they'd found the right thread. All they had to do was follow it back to the embezzler. The computer-made payments to Conway, Inc. had begun a little over a year before, weren't made with any regularity, and were never for an outstandingly large amount; but a few thousand here and there added up before long. All of the checks were on microfilm, but they were unable to get a signature from the canceled checks; they were all stamped with a rubber stamp that said DEPOSIT ONLY, CONWAY, INC. with the account number and bank name beneath it. Brett jotted down the number and bank.

"That's it until we can see the withdrawal slips, or the name on the checks written on that account." He had a headache from hours of staring at the bright green numbers on the display screen. Impatience rose up in him, impatience with both himself and the job, which grated on him increasingly as the days passed. Soon, he promised himself silently. Soon he would be on the ranch, and his fatigue would be the result of good, hard physical work, rather than from sitting hunched over faded computer printouts or working his way through the maze of computer programming, ferreting information out of electronic files.

"Let's pack it up and get some sleep."

Evan was more than willing, and the drive back to the hotel was accomplished in silence. In his room, Brett undressed and sprawled on the bed, almost groaning aloud as his tired muscles relaxed. The end was in his grasp now, and he wanted to get it over and done with; he wanted to put this behind him and get to the ranch. Funny, but years ago, when he'd been in college, the ranch hadn't pulled at him the way it was doing now. It had been home, but there had been an entire world out there that had challenged him, daring him to take his sharp, icy intellect and master it. He'd done it; he'd made a success of himself, using his cool grit and steely determination. He was not only very good at what he did, but he was well paid for it, too, and that had enabled him to invest, to diversify. His financial acumen had put the ranch on solid ground, much better able to weather the vagaries of the beef market than a lot of ranches. Tessa wouldn't be reminded of her youth, spent in a rundown old farmhouse. She'd still be able to wear silk, if she wanted it.

He closed his eyes, but her image filled his mind, and he opened them again, knowing that he wouldn't be able to sleep. His body burned, as if she were still lying against him, her arms and legs twined around him.

It was a hell of a coincidence that the embezzler had used Conway as a name.

His memory was almost photographic; abruptly he recalled Tessa's personnel file, and the dates of her employment. She'd been working at Carter Engineering for fifteen months. The embezzling had begun roughly thirteen months before. She worked in the bookkeeping department. And she was on very friendly terms with Sammy Wallace.

He swore aloud in the darkened room. Hell, what was he thinking? It wouldn't be Tessa; she was all sunlight and laughter. No, it would be Sammy Wallace, who'd probably picked Tessa's last name as some sort of twisted tribute. Like all men, Sammy Wallace could easily make a fool of himself where Tessa was concerned.

But, damn him, why did he have to drag her into his dirty little scheme? Didn't he realize that using her name would automatically make her the first suspect? Brett's mouth tightened. Of course he realized that! Why not try to throw the blame on Tessa? Wallace probably knew well enough that she would be less likely to be prosecuted than anyone else working at Carter Engineering.

He'd like to knock the bastard's teeth down his throat for putting her in jeopardy like that.

He was so tired that his entire body ached, and it was almost dawn, but he couldn't sleep. He kept thinking of Tessa, of the day he'd spent with her...mostly in bed. His good intentions hadn't been worth a damn when faced with the temptation of her body; he couldn't get enough of her. No matter how wild their lovemaking had been, he'd begun wanting her again as soon as it was over. Nothing in his previous experience had prepared him for the deep hunger he felt for her, and the inability to satisfy that hunger. But he'd tried, and she'd been sleeping in exhaustion when he left her, her dark hair spread in a wild tangle across the pillow.

The image haunted him. He turned restlessly on his stomach, bitter resentment rising in him again. He didn't like this compulsive need for her. He liked being in control, and with her he wasn't even in control of his own body, because he couldn't make himself stay away from her. He didn't like the power she had over him. He couldn't get her out of his mind! Even now, when he needed so badly to sleep, he remembered the feel of her silky body beneath him, the clasp of her legs around his hips, the deep, inner heat of her. His flesh stirred, and he swore between his teeth. Even in bed, she'd flirted and teased, laughing at him and moving elusively away from him. He'd been too sexually preoccupied to mention getting married, but soon he'd have to put an end to this damnable situation. When they were married, when he had her in his bed every night, she'd be his for good, and he'd be in control once more. With that on his mind, he went to sleep, but even in his sleep it seemed that he was tortured by the power she had over him, and fought with her for control of their relationship. He'd never felt so strongly about a woman before, and his feelings were both unexpected and unwelcome. In his life, he'd trusted only Tom, but now he had Tessa to deal with, and in her own way she was an enigma to him. She was both delicate and strong, elusive but his for the taking, yet even when he took her, he felt that there was a part of her that escaped him, and she was driving him crazy, even in his dreams.

When he woke, it was late in the afternoon; the first thing he thought was that Tessa must be wondering where the hell he was. He'd already picked up the receiver to call her before resentment rose in him. Damn it, he didn't have to check in with her like some grade-schooler! He dropped the receiver back into its cradle; then frustration with himself got the upper hand and he picked it up again, punching out Evan's room number. Evan answered on the third ring, his voice thick and still sleepy, and Brett knew that, like himself, Evan was catching up on his sleep. "I'm going over to Tessa's," he said brusquely. "You can get in touch with me there if you need me."

"Sure," Evan agreed sleepily, then laughed. "I don't blame you. If I could be with her, I wouldn't be wasting time in a hotel room, either!"

Brett showered and shaved, his lowered eyebrows testimony to his black mood. He was getting damned tired of every man in the country slavering over Tessa like dogs over a juicy bone. She was his. No other man had ever held her naked in his arms as he had done. With his hands and mouth and possessive lovemaking he'd branded her as his, every lovely, silky inch of her. He burned to have her again, to bury himself in her and hold her so close that nothing could get between them, to protect her from the undefined threat that was hanging over her head. He hoped that no one ever told her that she'd been used as a cover to hide an embezzler. She liked Sammy Wallace. She'd be distressed enough when he was arrested without knowing that he'd used her.

Half an hour later he rang her doorbell. Then impatience made him abandon the bell and bang on the door with his fist.

"Hold your horses!" he heard her mutter irritably on the other side of the door, and surprise at her bad mood made his eyebrows lift. "Who is it?"

"Me," he answered shortly.

The door didn't open, and she said just as shortly, "What do you want?"

The surge of anger that shook him was so strong that he ground his teeth in an effort to control it. What sort of game was she playing now? He wasn't going to argue with her through a door. "Tessa, open this door," he said in a controlled voice, then barked, *"Now!"*

She opened it, but blocked his entrance. Her face was cool and blank, but her eyes were spitting green fire. She didn't have any prior experience with love affairs, but she'd known immediately that she didn't like going to bed with her lover, the man she loved, and waking to an empty bed and an empty apartment, with no note to tell her where he was or when he would be back, with no phone call all day long. Brett Rutland was so arrogant that he probably expected her still to be waiting for him in bed where he'd left her.

He took a step forward, towering over her, but she didn't step back to let him in the door. His navy eyes narrowed. Did she expect to block him with her body? The idea was almost laughable, if he'd been in the mood to laugh. She barely reached his shoulder, and he outweighed her by at least a hundred pounds; he was roped with powerful muscles, while she was all soft silk and satin, yet she stood there glaring stubbornly up at him. Why had he never noticed the proud willfulness in her expression? She had a flashfire temper, he suddenly realized, a temper that was usually hidden behind lazy laughter, because she protected herself with indifference and humor. She became angry only when she cared about something.

She cared. Before she realized what he was about, he put his hand on her waist and gently lifted her to eye level with him, holding her suspended in the air. "I worked all night," he explained in a quiet, level tone. "Evan and I went to bed about dawn. When I woke up, I showered and shaved and came straight over here. I'm not used to anyone having the right to expect an explanation of my whereabouts."

Tessa still glowered at him. If that was supposed to be an apology, he needed a lot of work in that area; but then, it was really only an explanation, and a reluctantly given one at that. Still, in a back-ended way he'd admitted that she had the right to an explanation. The hard edge of her anger evaporated, but she wasn't able to forgive him completely yet.

"Put me down," she finally said, her voice as level as his.

"Kiss me, first."

She stared at him, then blushed. "No. If I do, you'll...we'll..."

A tiny smile of amusement curled his hard mouth. "Baby, I already am, and we will anyway."

She wanted to hit him. "You're not short in the ego department, are you?"

"Or any other department," he whispered, and eased her against him. "Put your legs around me."

Furiously she pushed against him. "Brett, we're standing in an open door! Put me down!"

He took another step forward and kicked the door shut behind him. "Tessa," he growled, and fastened his mouth to hers. Her hands were braced against his heavy shoulders, and she tried again to push herself away from him, again without result. His mouth was hot, moving on hers, opening her lips for the entry of his tongue, and she shuddered at the electric pleasure that jolted her body. With a whispery moan she stopped trying to hold on to her anger. Despite wanting to box his ears, she loved him, and loving him was so much better than fighting with him. He hadn't declared undying love and devotion, but still he'd given her more than any other woman had ever had from him. He'd given her the right to question him. She hadn't chosen a comfortable man to love, but he was all man, and she was going to make him all hers.

His breathing was heavy, his mouth hungry as he moved it down to her throat. Arching her against him with one hard arm clamped around her waist, he closed his other hand over her breast. Her legs parted automatically for him; she lifted them to clamp her thighs on either side of his lean waist, with her ankles locked behind him. "That's right," he rasped against her throat as he pushed himself against the cradle of her body. He kneaded her breast, wringing little cries of pleasure from her and making her writhe against him until he couldn't stand the sweet torment any longer and began walking toward the bedroom, still holding her wrapped tightly around him.

"Tell me that you love me," he demanded in a low, harsh whisper as he placed her on the bed and swiftly stripped away her clothes.

"I love you." She saw the flare of satisfaction in his eyes, satisfaction and something else, something cool and unreadable, and she was suddenly frightened. But then he was naked and he came down on the bed with her, covering her with his hard, heated flesh. He entered her at once, so powerfully that her nails sank into his shoulders. He made love to her with a passion that was almost violent, but always controlled, and he controlled her, too, setting their rhythm and pace, wringing sensations from her. He gave her exquisite pleasure, but even at the peak of her ecstasy, she wondered at the bitter look of resentment he'd given her.

Chapter Six

Brett stared at the microfilm of the checks written on the account of the bogus Conway, Inc. and sweat beaded on his forehead as he fought the urge to vomit. Nothing in his life had ever made him any sicker than he felt at the moment, and he closed his eyes, slumping weakly against the back of his chair. He couldn't take it in; he simply couldn't believe it, couldn't grasp the implications of it. The signature on the bottom of those checks was a very feminine one. An attempt had been made to disguise the handwriting by using a script that was a mixture of printing and writing, but that didn't matter. What mattered, what had hit him with such force that he felt as if he'd been pole-axed, was the

name: Tessa Conway. Tessa! God in heaven, how could
it be her? How could she cling to him as she had, give
herself so fiercely, whisper that she loved him, when all
the time she was stealing from the company that it was
his job to protect?

He raised a shaking hand to his eyes, as if to shield
them from the damning evidence before him, but he
couldn't shield himself from his own thoughts, and they
grew more bitter as the moments passed. He'd been
used, for a motive as old as time. Had she thought that
if she forged a relationship with him, he wouldn't be
able to prosecute her if her little get-rich-the-easy-way
scheme was uncovered? Had she thought that he might
even protect her? Damn her, she'd even given him her
virginity! She was a smart woman, all right. Few men
could cast off the entwined chains of guilt, responsibility and passion.

He'd made a fool of himself with her, he thought
bitterly. But at least he hadn't gotten around to asking
her to marry him. At least she didn't know just how big
a fool he was. That was the only consolation his pride
could find: She didn't know. Black rage boiled up in
him at the thought that she must be smugly congratu-
lating herself for luring him into her net so easily. It was
barely a week since he'd seen her for the first time, and
she'd had him tied in knots, ready to quit his job and
take her away with him to the ranch, full of stupid
dreams about the future with her as his wife, even
planning for the children they'd have.

The hell of it was, the signs had been there for him to read, if he hadn't been blinded by his own lust. She had both the skill and the opportunity. Her apartment, though not luxurious, certainly wasn't cheap. She drove a new car; she dressed well. She'd grown up in poverty, so much so that her aunt had had to take them in. Had she seen her thievery merely as insurance against a return to poverty?

The lying little bitch!

He shoved himself out of his chair and stood up, running his hand through his hair. He was shaking with the force of his fury, an anger so powerful that he could feel it burning inside him. No matter what her motive, she was a thief, and he was a fool. He'd been so hot for her that he'd neglected his job, something he'd never done before. It would be a long time before he allowed himself to forget that.

A knock on the door made him jerk around. He knew it would be Evan, so he said, "Come on in," and was amazed at the cool control in his voice.

"I couldn't get away from Ralph," Evan said as he entered and closed the door behind him. Ralph Little was head of data processing. "Did you get the microfilm of the checks?"

Brett indicated his desk. "Take a look."

Evan went over to the desk and looked at the copies of the checks. He was silent a moment, then rubbed the back of his neck. "Oh, hell," he said quietly.

Brett was silent.

Evan began to swear under his breath, a string of oaths that would have done credit to a sailor. He looked up at Brett, his eyes a little stunned. "This makes me sick."

His mouth twisting bitterly, Brett moved over to the window and looked out. "I know the feeling."

"Damn it, I never thought—not even when we caught on to that bogus account. I wrote it off as just a coincidence, or thought that the name had been picked because it was so similiar to Conmay."

"Yeah, so did I." He'd gotten control of himself, now that he was over the first brutal shock.

After a moment, Evan said, "What are you going to do?"

"Get a warrant for her arrest. Prosecute. Do the job I was sent down here to do."

The cold steel of Brett's voice made Evan wince. "Let's hold off for a few days; maybe if we talk to Mr. Carter—"

"His instructions are to prosecute to the full extent of the law. I intend to do just that."

"Brett, damn it, this is Tessa we're talking about!"

"I know exactly who we're talking about: a thief."

"I can't do it," Evan whispered.

There was nothing any colder than Brett's eyes. The expression in them was an arctic wasteland. "I can," he said.

He had to; he didn't have any choice about it. Nothing would ease the crippling sense of betrayal, the feeling that something vital had been torn out of his insides, but he could at least do the job he'd been sent to Los Angeles to do. He could refuse to make any more of a fool out of himself than he'd already done. In time, he might even be able to feel a little grateful to Tessa. After all, she'd shown him irrefutably that the best course was the one he'd always followed before her: Enjoy a woman, but don't allow her under your guard. He wouldn't make this mistake again. All he had to do now was his job...that, and get through the nights without her, when his body ached for her, when his mind was filled with the burning, erotic memories of making love to her.

Already he felt haunted. He pushed the thoughts of her away and strode to the desk to flick on the intercom. "Helen, get the D.A.'s office for me, please."

"The district attorney?" Helen asked in confirmation, her tone a little puzzled.

"That's right."

He turned the intercom off and met Evan's grim look.

"We've got all the evidence we need, though I'm going to have the handwriting of that signature analyzed, anyway," Evan said. "We can get a conviction, if that's what you're going after. But for God's sake, don't have her arrested here at work. Don't do that to her."

Brett's eyes went black. "I wasn't going to," he snapped. "Do you think I'd humiliate her that way?"

Suddenly pain sliced through him, and he closed his eyes for a moment. No, he didn't want to publicly humiliate her. He wanted to beat the living daylights out of her to teach her not to steal; then he wanted to chain her to his wrist and drag her off to Wyoming and keep her there for the rest of her life. Even now, even knowing how she'd used him, he wanted her, and admitting that to himself hurt as much as the knowledge that she'd been playing with him.

The intercom buzzed. "Mr. Rutland, I have John Morrison, the district attorney, on line one."

"Thank you, Helen." Brett punched the appropriate line, not even wondering how Helen had gotten the district attorney himself. He didn't care. All he could do now was concentrate on getting this done and over with, and living through it.

When he hung up the phone ten minutes later, he had a hollow feeling in the pit of his stomach. The wheels had been set in motion. Sweat beaded on his forehead, and he wiped it away. "We have to take all of this to the D.A.'s office," he said, indicating the damning copies of the checks, the piles of computer printouts, the lists of account numbers, all the methods they'd used to eliminate the legitimate withdrawals.

"Yeah. I'll do it." Evan's voice was hollow, and his face was gray. Brett wondered briefly what in hell he looked like, if Evan looked that bad. Evan knew her only peripherally, while he...God, he'd had her beneath him in bed, writhing in mindless need, her body sweet and hot and clinging, accepting his powerful thrusts with joyous abandon. At least he'd kept his head enough not to risk making her pregnant.... As soon as he had the thought, he went cold. Yesterday afternoon. He remembered standing in the doorway, lifting her up and clasping her to him. He remembered her legs locking around his waist. He'd carried her to bed, and in his urgency to possess her he hadn't thought about protecting her. Perhaps, in the back of his mind, he'd even discounted the need to do so, since he'd planned on marrying her so soon that any pregnancy would have been only a little early. But now...

Was this part of her scheme, too? She'd never even mentioned birth control. Had she deliberately ignored it, hoping that the possibility of her having his baby would force him to protect her if she got caught?

What the hell difference did it make? he wondered, agonized. If she was pregnant, whether it was deliberate or an accident, he'd have to protect her. He couldn't let his child be born in a prison hospital. He'd no longer have the option of quitting his job. He'd be fired for going behind Joshua Carter's back and dropping the charges against her, but he had the legal authority to do it, and he'd use it, if he had to. A bitter smile curved his mouth. It was a measure of how far down the road to madness he was that he found himself actually hoping that she was pregnant, so he'd have an excuse to step in and jerk her out of the mess she'd gotten herself into.

"Brett? Are you all right?"

Evan's reluctantly posed question brought him out of his black thoughts, and he realized that his fists were clenched. Slowly, he forced himself to relax. "I'm all right," he said, but his throat burned on the words, as if he'd screamed them instead. "Get this stuff down to the D.A.'s office, and let's get it over with."

Over lunch with Billie that day, Tessa couldn't keep the smile from her lips or the glow from her eyes. She was in love, and after yesterday she was certain that Brett loved her, too, even though he hadn't said it. She realized instinctively that the words would come hard to him; he'd be reluctant to admit his emotional vulnerability. His aloof, controlled character made it difficult for him to allow anyone to get close to him, but she no longer had any doubt that by some bright miracle she'd done exactly that. The thought of having that incredibly tough, sexy man love her made her feel oddly humble, for her life had been almost boringly mundane and normal, and she'd never done anything outstanding or exalted enough to earn his love. She wasn't a high-powered executive or lawyer, or a passionately dedicated doctor, or a brilliantly talented artist. She was a bookkeeper, and content with her position in life, for she lacked intense ambition in her character makeup. Her only gifts were laughter and the ability to enjoy life. Why was that enough to attract a man like him? And did she really care, so long as he *was* attracted? Of course not!

First Class Romance

Delivered to your door by

Silhouette Special Edition®

(See inside for special 4 FREE book offer)

Find romance at your door with 4 FREE novels from Silhouette Special Edition!

Slip away to a world that's only as far away as your mailbox. A world of romance, where the pace of life is as gentle as a kiss, and as fast as the pounding of a lover's heartbeat. Wrap yourself in the special pleasure of having Silhouette Special Edition novels arrive at your home.

By filling out and mailing the attached postage-paid order card you'll receive FREE 4 new Silhouette Special Edition romances and a Cameo Tote Bag (a $16.99 value).

You'll also receive an extra bonus: our monthly Silhouette Books Newsletter. Then approximately every 4 weeks we'll send you six more Silhouette Special Edition romances to examine FREE for 15 days. If you decide to keep them, you'll pay just $11.70 (a $15.00 value) with no extra charge for home delivery and at no risk! You'll have the option to cancel at any time. Just drop us a note. Your first 4 books and the Tote Bag are yours to keep in any case.

Silhouette Special Edition

EXTRA BONUS
A Free Cameo Tote

You'll receive brand-new
novels as they're published!

Mail this card today for your
4 FREE BOOKS
and this Tote Bag
(a $16.99 value)!

FILL OUT THIS POSTCARD AND MAIL TODAY!

Silhouette Special Edition®

Silhouette Books, 120 Brighton Rd., P.O. Box 5084, Clifton, NJ 07015-9956

☐ Yes, please send 4 new Silhouette Special Edition novels and Cameo Tote Bag to my home FREE and without obligation. Unless you hear from me after I receive my 4 FREE books, please send me 6 new Silhouette Special Edition novels for a free 15-day examination each month as soon as they are published. I understand that you will bill me a total of just $11.70 (a $15.00 value) with no additional charges of any kind. There is no minimum number of books that I must buy, and I can cancel at any time. No matter what I decide, the first 4 books and Cameo Tote Bag are mine to keep.

NAME _____

(please print)

ADDRESS _____

CITY _____ STATE _____ ZIP _____

Terms and prices subject to change.
Your enrollment is subject to acceptance by Silhouette Books.

Silhouette Special Edition is a registered trademark.

CAS325

She was so full of happiness that when the waiter rather sloppily served their food, she overflowed with joy and rewarded him with a smile that stopped him in his tracks, and he retreated with a rather stunned look on his face.

"You look happy," Billie understated dryly.

"Do I?" Happy wasn't the way she felt; she felt delirious with joy.

"The waiter's tongue is hanging out." Then Billie laughed. "I take it you had an enjoyable weekend?"

"I never thought it would happen this fast," Tessa mused, answering Billie's question obliquely. "I thought that it would grow gradually, like a building going up brick by brick."

"Brett Rutland doesn't look like the type to have any patience with the brick-by-brick method. I never should have doubted you. The poor guy didn't have a chance. Rather than warning you, I should've been warning him. So when's the wedding?"

"We haven't discussed that," Tessa answered serenely, never doubting that the subject would be discussed before too much longer. "If he can get away this weekend, he's taking me to his ranch in Wyoming."

"Oh, ho! To meet the family?"

"His father, anyway. They own the ranch together. He hasn't mentioned any other family."

"No problem, then. Well, whaddaya know?" Billie sighed in intense satisfaction. "We have great timing. Both of us, in the same weekend."

Surprised, Tessa looked at Billie's bright, smiling face, then glanced quickly at Billie's left hand. A sparkling diamond adorned it. She shrieked, then jumped up to pull Billie out of her chair and hug her. "You sneak!" she chortled. "You didn't even tell me you were getting serious about anyone! Well, who is it? David? Ron? No, I know, don't tell me! I know!"

"You do not," Billie laughed, ignoring the scene they were making in the restaurant.

"Patrick!"

"How did you know?" Billie yelped; then they were hugging each other again.

"This calls for a toast," Tessa proclaimed, picking up her glass of bottled water with the twist of lime that she liked in it. "To Billie and Patrick!"

"To Tessa and Brett!" Billie picked up her teacup, and they clicked cup and glass together, then drank toasts to each other. When they resumed their seats, Billie said, "Well, how did you know?"

"Elementary, my dear Billingsley." Tessa sniffed. "Patrick is obviously smarter than the other two."

Billie had been dating Patrick Hamilton, as well as her other two suitors, for almost a year, but she'd never revealed any partiality to any of them. In Tessa's opinion, though, Patrick was definitely the best man for Billie. He was a civil engineer, more at home in jeans and a hard hat than he'd ever be in a suit, but with a self-assured masculinity that would do wonders to Billie's rather delicate ego.

"Thanks," Billie said softly. "What would I have done without you?"

"Met and married him anyway. I told you, Patrick is smart."

"He'd never even looked at me twice before you came along and stopped me from looking like an escapee from a punk rock concert. I knew what you were doing, but I pretended not to notice," Billie admitted a little shyly. "When Patrick asked me out, I had to pinch myself so I'd know it was real. I mean, look at him! And look at me. I couldn't believe it; I didn't even let myself hope. But this weekend...well, he'll be leaving the country on a job that'll keep him gone for almost two years, and he...he put this ring on my finger and flatly informed me that there was no way in hell—his words—he was going to spend two years without me, so I'd have to quit my job and go to Brazil with him." She grinned. "I almost sprained my tongue, I said yes so fast. I'll be turning in my notice at the end of this month."

They were so caught up in their celebrating that they were almost late getting back to work, and Tessa sailed through the rest of the day on a cloud. Brett hadn't called her to make plans for the night, but somehow she hadn't expected him to. Their relationship had progressed to the point that she felt he knew she wouldn't have any other plans, just as she knew that she'd see him that night. She didn't even feel a twinge of regret when she turned down invitations from two men she liked very much. They simply weren't Brett.

After work, she rushed home and took a pack of beef tips out of the freezer section of the refrigerator, putting it in the sink to thaw. She didn't know what sort of work Brett was doing, but she'd seen the strain of it in his face when he'd shown up yesterday afternoon. He was tired; if he wanted dinner, they'd eat there. And if he had to work, she had to have dinner anyway, she thought philosophically, though she felt lonely at the mere thought of not seeing him that night.

She stopped in the middle of the kitchen floor, her eyes dreamy, her pulse speeding up. Until she'd met him, she hadn't known she could be so sensual, but all she had to do was look at him to feel her body heating. She wanted him with an intensity that was alarming, because her life had become focused on him to the exclusion of all else. His lovemaking made her go out of her mind with feverish desire. She couldn't control it, didn't even want to control it. She just wanted to lie with him every night for the rest of her life. She wanted to have his children, fight with him, love with him, ride beside him on his ranch, flirt with him until his beautiful navy eyes smoldered with desire and he reached out for her in compulsive need. She couldn't wait to tell Aunt Silver—

Silver! Groaning, Tessa remembered that an airmail letter from Silver had been in her mailbox, but she'd been in such a hurry to get the beef tips out of the freezer that she'd just thrown everything on the couch and gone straight to the kitchen. After retracing her steps to the living room, she sorted through her mail, picking out the letter from Silver and tearing it open.

Smiling, she read the long, newsy letter. The mountains were full of blooms, and the summer crowds had already begun pushing into Gatlinburg. The doll shop was doing so well that Silver had hired extra help, and she'd been approached by a man who wanted to buy the old farm in Sevierville, if Tessa was interested in selling her half.

Silver didn't mention Brett until the last paragraph, but Tessa laughed out loud when she read it. She'd known Silver's instinct would zoom in on him like steel to a magnet. "Bring this Brett Rutland to see me," Silver instructed in her letter. "Your handwriting shook when you wrote his name!"

The doorbell rang, and still chuckling, Tessa laid the letter aside. Her heart had already begun racing when she opened the door, expecting Brett. But it wasn't Brett who stood there. She didn't know the man and woman who faced her. "Teresa Conway?" the woman asked.

"Yes. Can I help you?"

The woman opened the flap of her purse, exhibiting a badge. "I'm Detective Madison, from the L.A.P.D. This is Detective Warnick. We have a warrant for your arrest."

It was late that night when Tessa let herself back into her apartment, and she groped her way through the dark to the couch, not even thinking to turn on any lights. She sat down, Silver's discarded letter crinkling under her, and she automatically removed the sheets of paper. Fine tremors shook her entire body, and she couldn't stop them. She'd been shaking for hours, ever since the nightmare had begun. This wasn't happening to her; it couldn't be happening. She hadn't believed Detective Madison, at first. She'd actually laughed, wanting to know who was behind the joke. Detective Warnick had read her her rights, gently but inexorably insisted that she get her purse and come with them, and still Tessa hadn't believed it was anything serious. It wasn't until she was escorted outside and put in the back seat of what was obviously an unmarked police car that she'd been struck with the realization that this was no joke, and it was then that she'd begun shaking.

She'd been arrested for embezzling. She'd understood that much of what they'd told her. They'd told her a lot, but though she'd tried very hard to concentrate, most of it hadn't made any sense. She was too frightened, too stunned to take it in. The police station had been a buzz of activity, with people coming and going and not paying any attention to her, but she'd been taken through the process of being booked with a casual sort of professionalism that chilled her. She'd been fingerprinted, and her picture taken, and both questioned and advised. Someone had given her a tissue to wipe the black ink from her fingertips, and she'd devoted herself to that task. It had been of paramount importance to clean the stain from her hands.

Finally, the thought had been born that she should call Brett. He'd get her out of this nightmare. At the thought of him, she'd become calm. There was nothing that Brett couldn't handle. He'd sort out this mistake, because that was obviously all it was. But what if he weren't at his hotel? What if he were waiting at her apartment, growing more and more furious because she wasn't there? What if he thought she'd gone out with some other man—which she had, in a way. She almost giggled, thinking of the way Detective Warnick had held her arm as they walked out to the car.

But she'd called his hotel anyway, only to be told that Mr. Rutland had given instructions that no calls were to be put through to him. Tessa tried to explain that it was an emergency, but the hotel operator couldn't be budged. In desperation, she asked for Evan Brady's room. He could take a message to Brett, if Brett was tied up with work.

Evan had answered on the second ring, and in a stumbling rush, Tessa explained who she was and that she needed to talk to Brett. There had been a long pause, then Evan had said evenly, "He knows."

Tessa's fingers had been shaking so much that she'd almost dropped the telephone. "Wh—what?" she stammered. "How...no, that doesn't matter. When will he be here?"

"I...ah...don't think he will."

That didn't make sense. Tessa closed her eyes, fighting down the nausea that had been threatening for some time. "What do you mean? You don't understand what I'm talking about—"

"Yes, I understand." The disembodied voice in her ear became a little rougher. "Miss Conway...Tessa...Brett is the one who filed the charges against you."

Had he said anything after that? She didn't know. She'd simply taken the phone from her ear and sat there with the receiver clutched in her hand so tightly that her fingers had turned white, until Detective Warnick had gently removed the instrument from her grasp and offered, probably against all regulations, to call someone else for her. She'd refused, her mind blank, her emotions numb. Who else was there to call? What did it matter, anyway?

She hadn't seen the faintly concerned glances that passed between Detectives Madison and Warnick. She hadn't seen anything unusual in the Styrofoam cup of very strong, black coffee that was pressed into her grasp. She hadn't drunk it, but had held it, grateful for the warmth it brought to her chilled hands.

She'd been told that the court would appoint an attorney for her, if she couldn't afford one, and she'd frowned in a puzzled manner. "I can afford a lawyer," she said mildly, and gone back to examining the odd swirls of color on top of the black coffee.

She'd been allowed to sign her own bond, and she'd done so, but though she was then free to go, it hadn't seemed very important to her, and she'd continued to sit there in the hard, uncomfortable chair. When Detective Madison's shift had ended at eleven, she'd shepherded Tessa out to her own car, and that was how Tessa had gotten home.

She couldn't think. Unformed words swirled in her mind, but she couldn't grasp them long enough to make anything coherent of them. At last, moving slowly and jerkily, she curled up in a ball on the couch, as if to protect herself from the pain that awaited her if she ever allowed herself to notice it. It was there, hovering just on the edge of her consciousness, like a savage animal crouched in readiness to spring on her and claw her to shreds. If she just didn't let herself look at it, if she didn't admit its presence to herself, she'd be safe. She'd be safe. Telling herself that, she sank into the comforting blackness of sleep.

It was daylight when she woke, and she surged to her feet, her mind thick with sleep but recognizing instinctively that it was late. She had to hurry, or she'd be late to work. Tearing off her wrinkled clothing as she stumbled to the bathroom, not even questioning why she'd been sleeping on the couch, she was actually under the shower before she remembered what had happened the night before. Her lips trembled as she sagged against the wall of the shower. Late for work? The guard probably had express orders not to let her inside the building! If there was anything she could count on, it was that she no longer had a job.

It was then that the first tears came, and she cried helplessly as she automatically soaped and rinsed herself. How had this happened? It didn't make any sense. She'd never stolen anything. Didn't Brett know that? He had to know that! Unless someone had deliberately made it look as if she'd been embezzling—of course, what else could it be? She had to talk to Brett. If he thought she'd been stealing, there had to be some pretty strong evidence against her, but she'd make him believe her.

Rushing now, she turned off the shower and dried off, then wrapped the towel around her and stumbled to the phone, punching out the numbers for Carter Engineering. She was put through to Brett's office without any trouble, and her spirits took a crazy upward swing. But when Helen Weis answered the phone, and Tessa asked for Brett, Helen hesitated.

"I'm sorry," Helen finally said. "Mr. Rutland isn't taking any calls."

"Please," Tessa begged. "This is Tessa Conway. I have to speak to him!"

"I'm sorry," Helen repeated. "He expressly said that he wouldn't take any calls from you."

Tessa was trembling again as she hung up the phone. What was she going to do now? What could she do? Brett wouldn't talk to her, and in the face of that she was lost.

Several minutes later, she took a deep breath and straightened her spine. No, she wasn't lost. She couldn't get through to Brett on the phone. She'd see him in person, at his hotel, this evening. She wasn't going to let him go on thinking that she was a thief. She wouldn't even let herself believe that he'd been the one to press charges against her until he told her so himself. In the meantime, she had to take steps to protect herself. She'd been in shock, but she wasn't helpless, and she wasn't going to let herself be railroaded into prison for something she hadn't done. Her first step was to hire a lawyer, and the best place to find one was the telephone book.

By mid-afternoon, she'd secured the legal services of Calvin R. Stine and had a long meeting with him. He'd turned out to be a sharp-eyed man in his early thirties, just beginning to establish himself as a trial lawyer. He'd taken down a lot of information, most of which had seemed irrelevant to Tessa, but she'd willingly answered all his questions. He'd also told her what to expect. Her case, being a felony, would be brought before a grand jury, who would consider the evidence and decide if the State of California had sufficient evidence against her to warrant a trial. If the grand jury decided that there was insufficient evidence, all charges against her would be dropped.

Tessa pinned her hopes on that. If she had to go on trial...somehow, she didn't think she could stand it.

When she finally left Mr. Stine's office, she felt so weak that she could barely walk, and with faint surprise she realized that she hadn't eaten since lunch the day before, when she and Billie had laughed and toasted each other. How brightly the sun had shone on her barely twenty-four hours before! But everything was gray now, she thought, not noticing the gorgeous Southern Californian spring day.

She had to eat something, but it was getting close to the time when Brett would return to his hotel, and she didn't want to miss him. The best thing to do, she decided, was to go to his hotel and get something to eat in the coffee shop there.

She did exactly that, but when her club sandwich was set before her, she could only pick at it. Every bite she took expanded in her mouth as she chewed it, and it was as tasteless as sawdust. Doggedly she forced herself to swallow a little of it, then picked the lettuce off and ate it a shred at a time while she nursed her glass of mineral water and checked the time every few minutes. Would Brett leave work promptly at five o'clock? She hadn't known him long enough to know his personal habits, she realized with a sharp pang. She hadn't known him long enough for him to believe without question that she wasn't capable of embezzlement.

Finally, when the waitress began giving her suspicious looks, Tessa decided to try her luck. If he wasn't in his room yet, she'd simply wait in the lobby for a while, then try again. Fortunately, she didn't have to ask for his room number; he'd given it to her the week before, in case she'd wanted to get in touch with him.

Her knees were shaking so badly that she had to cling to the rail in the elevator as it rose through the building, and they were still shaking as she searched for his room. When she finally found it, she froze before the blank door. What if he wouldn't let her in? Taking several deep breaths, she rapped sharply on the panel.

Evidently he was expecting someone, for he opened the door without checking. He went very still, staring down at her, and his rough-hewn face was contemptuous. "Somehow, I didn't expect you to force yourself in here," he said coldly.

"I have to talk to you," Tessa said in desperation, almost crying at the look on his face.

"Is it really necessary?" His voice was laced with boredom. "You won't accomplish anything, except to waste my time."

"I have to talk to you," she repeated, and with a sigh he stepped back, opening the door wider.

"Get it over with, then."

She entered the room, fingering her purse nervously. She'd planned to tell him immediately that she wasn't guilty, but now that she faced him and could see the distaste in his eyes, as if she'd brought a foul smell into the room with her, she couldn't quite do it. He didn't look like a man in pain, a man who'd been forced to do something that had to be almost as traumatic for him as it had been for her. He looked as cool and controlled as he'd ever been. There was no hint in his eyes that he even remembered the hours of lovemaking between them.

She stopped in the middle of the room and forced her hands to cease their nervous movements. "Evan Brady—" Her voice was raw and shaky and she stopped, clearing her throat. "Evan Brady told me that you're the one who pressed charges against me."

"That's right," Brett said easily, moving away from her and settling himself against the edge of the writing desk in front of the windows. He stretched out his long legs, crossing them negligently at the ankle.

"You didn't even warn me—"

He burst out laughing, a cold, contemptuous laugh that flayed her skin, making her wince. "Did you think that just because we had sex together, I'd be so wild about you that I'd let you get away with theft? You're a good lay, honey, I'll give you that, but I had a job to do."

Tessa stared at him, her breathing stopped in her chest, though her heart was pounding so heavily that the sound of it filled her head. He couldn't be saying those things! She was as still and pale as a statue, only her burning eyes alive as she looked at him. Slowly she went over his words, feeling something die inside of her. Her tongue was stiff and didn't want to work, but she forced the words out. "Did you...are you saying that the only reason you asked me out...the only reason..."

"You made our investigation easy," he said, and smiled. "Maybe I shouldn't have taken advantage of the fringe benefits you offered, but you're a sexy little thing, and I wanted you to feel secure enough that you wouldn't bolt." Clenching his jaw with the effort it cost him to smile, he mentally thanked her for giving him the excuse herself. He couldn't let her see that she'd almost brought him to his knees. If nothing else, he had to hang on to his pride. God, she was lovely, and so delicate that it was almost impossible to believe her capable of embezzlement, even though he'd seen the evidence himself.

"One other thing," he said, disguising his bitterness with a casual tone. "You made me lose my head Sunday afternoon, and I forgot to take care of things. It's not likely, but if you're pregnant, let me know. Damn it, even knowing you probably did it deliberately, a pregnancy would change things," he admitted reluctantly.

Tessa hadn't moved an inch. Her face was paper white. "No, I don't think it would change anything at all," she said, and walked out.

Chapter Seven

Tessa had been hurt before, but nothing had ever made her feel as she did when she walked out of Brett's hotel room. It was a pain so deep, so crippling, that she couldn't even imagine the scope of it, yet in a way it was also a blessing, because the shock of it numbed her. He not only didn't love her, but also had been using her all along! She'd thought that they'd had something real, something infinitely precious between them, only to find that he'd sought her out for his investigation. The love she'd been so certain of had existed only in her mind. If he felt anything at all for her, it was only lust. He'd used her body only because she'd offered it, and it had meant nothing to him beyond momentary physical pleasure.

Now, with the wisdom of hindsight, she remembered all the casual questions he'd asked her the first time he'd taken her out to dinner. A harsh laugh tore from her throat. She'd thought he was making conversation, an easy way of getting to know her, but instead he'd been digging for information!

She felt...dirty. The horror of being arrested, of being fingerprinted, hadn't made her feel that way, because she'd known herself to be innocent of the charge they'd made against her, of the charge that *Brett* had filed against her. But now she felt violated, both mentally and physically. She'd given her love to him in every way she knew, openly, trustingly, and he'd used her as casually as any whore had ever been used. He'd turned his back on her, not caring that he'd trampled on her emotions, not caring that she felt soiled and lifeless.

There was a lump in her throat that felt as if it were choking her. She swallowed convulsively, looking around in mild surprise. She was in her own apartment, and she had no remembrance of getting there. She didn't remember anything from the moment she'd left Brett's hotel room, though the clock on the wall told her that so little time had elapsed that she must have come straight home.

There had been times in the past when she'd felt beaten down, but she'd always recovered, always found again the ability to laugh and enjoy life. Perhaps laughter was beyond her now, but there was steel in her, steel that wouldn't allow her to knuckle under. She wasn't going to go tamely to prison for something she hadn't done, even if Brett Rutland had torn her heart out. She'd do whatever she could to prove her innocence. He could break her only if she allowed him to, and she wasn't going to do that. All she had left now was her pride, and the knowledge of her innocence; with that, she'd survive. She had to turn her back on her pain, push Brett out of her mind, because if she allowed her tortured thoughts to dwell on him, she'd go mad.

With that decision, it was as if a door had slammed in her mind. Her face was calm as she went to the phone. She wanted the one person who would never turn against her.

"Honey, it's so nice to hear your voice!" Silver exclaimed happily, hundreds of miles and three time zones away. "I was just thinking about you. Are you calling about wedding plans?"

"No," Tessa said calmly. "Aunt Silver, I've been arrested. I need you."

Five minutes later, when Tessa hung up the phone, it was with Silver's grim reassurance ringing in her ears that she would be there the next day. If Tessa had needed an example of love and trust to compare with Brett's behavior, Silver had given it to her. Her aunt's support had been immediate and unquestioning, and so fierce that if Silver had been able to get her hands on Brett Rutland at that moment, he'd have been mauled before he'd even had the chance to protect himself.

She'd barely hung up the phone when her doorbell rang. Remembering the night before when she'd opened the door to the two detectives, an especially cruel shock when she'd been anticipating Brett's arrival so eagerly, Tessa froze for a moment. Had something gone wrong? Could her bond be rescinded?

"Tessa? Are you all right?"

It was Billie's voice, and she sounded anxious. As Tessa opened the door to her friend, she wondered how much Billie knew, if it was common knowledge at the office yet that she'd been arrested.

Billie's eyes were worried as she stepped into the apartment. "Are you sick?" she asked. "No one knew why you weren't at work today. I tried calling you at lunch, but there wasn't any answer."

"Would you like a cup of coffee?" Tessa offered, her voice calm and flat. Billie had already answered one of her questions: The reason for her absence hadn't been made public yet, though of course it would be, eventually. Gossip had a way of filtering out, like fine dust through the cracks in a floor.

"I'd like an answer, but I'll take a cup of coffee, too," Billie replied testily.

Well, why not? Why should she evade the issue? She hadn't done anything wrong. "I've been fired, I think." A faintly wry smile curved her lips. She hadn't actually received a dismissal, but then a warrant for her arrest had been pretty effective.

Following her into the kitchen, Billie stuttered questions at her. "Fired? Don't be ridiculous— What are you talking about? Why would anyone want to fire you? And what about Brett?"

Taking the coffee can down from the cabinet, Tessa calmly went about the process of making coffee. "Brett had me arrested," she stated from a remote sea of indifference. "For embezzlement. Turns out he was only interested in me from an investigative standpoint."

She turned and watched Billie, wondering if her offhand statement would spell the end of their friendship. At this point, she didn't have much faith in anyone, except Silver.

Billie flushed a dark red. "Are you for real?" she demanded in a harsh tone.

Tessa didn't say anything, but evidently the look on her pale, expressionless face convinced Billie. "Why that blind, conniving bastard!" Billie snarled, her small hands balling into fists. "You're no more a thief than...than my mother is! Where did he get a screwball idea like that? What sort of evidence does he have?"

"I don't know. I hired a lawyer today; I suppose he'll find out." A part of her frozen heart was warmed by Billie's instant defense, but it was a small part. The greater portion of her heart had died about an hour before.

Billie looked at Tessa, seeing the emptiness in her friend's eyes, and her lips trembled. "Oh, God, I can't stand this," she whispered, reaching out to hug Tessa tightly. "You were so happy, and for him to hit you between the eyes like this...I'm turning in my notice tomorrow! I'm not working for a monster like that!"

"I'll be all right," Tessa said quietly. "I know that I'm innocent; that's the most important thing. There's no need for you to quit because of me. You'll need your salary for all the things you'll have to buy when you and Patrick get married."

"But—"

"Please. It isn't necessary."

She eventually convinced Billie not to quit her job, but Billie's red-headed temper was aroused, and she stormed around the apartment, alternately threatening Brett with dismemberment and feverishly planning any defense Tessa could use. Tessa remained quiet, not really paying attention. She was interested in the future only in an abstract way, because she didn't have a real future anymore. Even if she cleared her name—no, *when* she cleared it—she would still be only half alive, going through the motions of living without feeling any of the joy, an empty shell that held only the echo of laughter.

When Billie calmed down, she and Tessa sat at the table and drank coffee. Billie tried to cheer Tessa up, and Tessa tried to respond, if only to ease Billie's mind, but the subject was like a sore tooth. No matter how they tried to talk about something else, they kept coming back to worry at it.

"There hasn't been a breath of this in the office," Billie said incredulously. "I'd swear that even Perry doesn't know about it."

Her eyes bitter, Tessa said, "I'm not going to try to cover it up. I'm not a thief, and I'm not going to act as if I'm guilty. Perhaps Brett and Evan have their reasons for keeping it quiet, but as far as I'm concerned, let everyone know about it, and let them know that I intend to fight this down to the last pea in the dish."

"You want me to let it out?" Billie asked incredulously.

"Why not? You know the old saw about the best defense—"

"Is a good offense. Gotcha. You're going to give him something to think about, right?"

"I don't care what he thinks. I'm fighting for my life," Tessa said flatly.

When Billie had gone, Tessa very carefully went around the apartment and made certain everything was locked, but even then she felt vulnerable and exposed, as if there were prying eyes looking through the walls. She had a horrible thought: Had the place been bugged? Wildly she looked around, before common sense reassured her that such measures would hardly be employed in her case. She forced herself to shower and get ready for bed, but when she went into the bedroom she stopped in her tracks, staring at the bed. There was no way she could sleep in that bed. Brett had slept in it with her, initiated her into the searing intimacies of lovemaking, held her through the night—and it had all been lies. The love she'd been so certain of had been a mirage, a false image projected to gain her confidence. There had been no security in his arms, only lies.

Shaking, she grabbed an extra blanket and returned to the living room, curling up on the couch as she'd done the night before. Lying there in the dark, staring into the darkness with wide, empty eyes, she wondered when she'd feel the first stirring of anger. Why couldn't she be angry? With anger would come strength, strength that she needed, but the only emotion she could feel was the hollow pain of betrayal, and that pain was too deep even for tears. She'd cried once, that morning in the shower, but somehow that seemed as if it had happened years ago, to someone else. This morning, even though she'd known then that Brett had been involved in her arrest, she'd still given him the benefit of the doubt. She'd hurt, but she'd also thought that he would be hurting, too, that he'd been faced with evidence so strong that he'd been forced to take action against her. Without even consciously thinking about it, she'd already forgiven him, because she loved him so much. This morning, she'd still been able to hope.

Now there was nothing for her except a bleak stretch of years. After Andrew, even in the depths of her bitterness, she'd somehow known that there would be sunny times ahead for her. She hadn't been broken; she'd been furious and hurt, but never broken, because she hadn't loved Andrew deeply enough that his betrayal could slash her heart. Well, the party girl was finally paying off all her old debts to fate. She'd waltzed away relatively unscathed too many times, but she wouldn't waltz away from this one. Even proving her innocence wouldn't change the fact that Brett didn't love her, and had never loved her.

She'd been too certain of her own charms, she realized bitterly; it was poetic justice. She was so used to men falling all over themselves for her that it had never entered her mind that Brett Rutland wasn't going to do the same. All her life, she'd been able to get around men with her slow smile and a flutter of her long lashes, but Brett Rutland was pure steel, and he'd probably smiled coldly to himself as he wound her around his little finger, all the while allowing her to believe that she was the one doing the charming.

But, dear God, she'd never been malicious in her flirting! Had she really deserved this?

It was the blackest night of her life, worse even than the one before. At least then she'd been numb and had eventually slept. There was no sleep for her tonight. She lay awake, chilled even beneath the blanket, and none of the prayers she sent up in any way lightened the darkness in her heart. Her heart beat slowly, heavily, as if it would never again race with joy or pound with excitement at being in the arms of the man she loved.

At dawn, she got up and prepared breakfast, but could force herself to eat only a slice of toast. It was hours yet before Silver's plane was due in, yet she had nothing else to do to pass the time. She dressed and drove to L.A. International, where she sat for hours in a coffee shop drinking cup after cup of coffee until her stomach was upset and she was forced to buy a roll of antacid tablets. Her mind was blank of all thoughts except the most superficial ones as she sat in the uncomfortable seat and waited for Silver's plane.

It landed at one-thirty, and she was waiting when Silver came out of the tunnel. As soon as she saw her aunt, Tessa felt some of the burden ease from her shoulders, and she actually smiled.

"Tessa, honey." Silver's warm, throaty voice, so much like Tessa's own, sounded in her ear as loving arms enveloped her, and the two women hugged each other with the fierceness of family love and loyalty.

"I'm glad you're here," Tessa said simply.

"You knew I'd come, and I'll stay as long as you need me. Gatlinburg can get along without me for a while."

They retrieved Silver's suitcase, and by the time they'd reached the car, Silver was making plans. She wasn't going to let her beloved niece be railroaded into jail without a fight that would make Brett Rutland think he'd caught a wildcat by the tail, with no way to turn it loose. The first thing to do was see this lawyer Tessa had hired and judge for herself if he was capable of fighting as fiercely for Tessa as he should.

By noon, there wasn't a person working for Carter Engineering who didn't know that Tessa Conway had been arrested for embezzlement, and Brett was coldly furious. Damn it, he'd done everything he could to keep it quiet for as long as possible. Despite what she'd done, he wanted to spare Tessa as much as he could. The knowledge that he wouldn't be able to protect her from the worst ate at him, like a gnawing animal inside. He hadn't even been able to keep gossip down for a measly two days. The only person who knew, besides himself, was Evan, though Helen was too smart not to have figured out most of it by now. But when he questioned them, they both denied breathing a word to anyone else. Helen eyed his stony face warily. She'd never before seen a man look so deadly. "I've been asked about it by at least ten different people this morning," she said. "Do you want me to try to track it down? Someone had to tell them."

"Find out," Brett said in a clipped tone.

Helen was competent enough and determined enough that Brett had no doubt that she'd be able to trace the gossip to its source before the day was out, and he only hoped he'd feel calmer by the time he knew the person's identity. But, damn it, who else could know?

He'd never been the most popular guy around. His job made that impossible, and his aloof personality only increased the distance between himself and the people he dealt with. But he'd never before felt himself to be so violently unpopular as he had that morning. People all over the building were glaring at him, including the guard. Tessa's charm had bubbled out and touched everyone she met, blinding them so that they were ready to ignore any evidence and rush to her defense.

Less than an hour later, Martha Billingsley, Tessa's friend, stood in his office with her arms crossed and her face hostile. "I heard that you're trying to find out how the news got out," she said coldly. "I did it."

Brett got to his feet, towering over the small redhead, who nevertheless continued to glare up at him. "I thought you were her friend," he snapped.

"I am. Friend enough that I want everyone to know what a raw deal she got. Tessa never stole a penny in her life. If you don't like what I'm saying, then fire me."

"Who told you about it?" he asked, ignoring her last statement.

"Tessa."

Somehow, he hadn't expected that. He'd have thought Tessa would try to keep it as quiet as she could. "She called you?"

"No. I went to her apartment last night."

His fist slowly clenched. Her face, when she'd left his hotel room, had been white and blank. Her last words had gone around and around in his mind, but still he couldn't pin down her meaning. *No, I don't think it would change anything at all,* she'd said, her voice remote, and she'd turned and quietly left. Did she mean that she thought he'd go through with the prosecution even if she were pregnant? She'd been so pale that he'd started to go after her, but his pride had stopped him. He wouldn't chase after her like a dog after a bitch in heat, not after he knew her for a liar and a thief.

"How was she?" he asked rawly, unable to stop the words.

Billie gave him a scathing look. "What do you care?"

"Damn it, how was she?" he roared, a muscle jerking in his cheek as he felt his control breaking.

It wasn't in Billie's pugnacious character to back down. "If you're so interested, go see for yourself, though I doubt Tessa would let you in the door." She stormed out, and even slammed the door behind her. Brett itched to grab the little red-headed wildcat and shake her, but at the same time he felt a grudging respect for her. Few people stood up to him at all.

Restlessly he paced over to the window. What sort of game was Tessa playing now? Did she think that if she stirred up enough support in the ranks at Carter Engineering, the charges against her would be dropped? Who knew what went on in her mind? She was a thief, a woman skilled enough at deceit that he'd been totally taken in by her until the evidence had forced him to accept the truth. She was capable of such a high degree of duplicity that the two images he had of her still warred in his mind. He simply couldn't blend them together into a single person.

And he wanted her. Heaven help him, he still wanted her.

Tessa stripped the bed and put clean sheets on it. "You can have the bed," she told Silver calmly. "I'll sleep on the couch."

"I'll do no such thing," Silver retorted, helping Tessa smooth the sheets. "I'll take the couch."

"It'll be crowded, with both of us on the couch," Tessa said. She didn't look up. "I can't sleep in here. I've been sleeping on the couch since—"

She broke off, her hands busy, and Silver watched her niece worriedly. Tessa had changed, and it wasn't simply that she was distraught at being arrested, though that was enough to make anyone a nervous wreck. But Tessa wasn't nervous; she was calm, unnaturally so. The sparkle that had always lit her from the inside was gone. Silver didn't want to think that it had been extinguished permanently, but she'd never seen Tessa like this before, not even after Andrew.

Silver looked at the bed, then back at Tessa. "He seduced you, didn't he?"

"At the time, I thought he was making love," Tessa said, after a silent moment. She smiled at Silver, but the smile didn't reach her eyes. "I'll be all right. At least I'm not pregnant."

"Are you sure?"

"Yes. This morning." Brett didn't have anything to worry about now. He could prosecute her with a clear conscience. Then she shoved him out of her mind, because she couldn't think about him any longer without breaking down, something that she refused to do. She had to keep the pain at bay, or she wouldn't be able to function. To that end, she kept her thoughts concerned only with the present. Rehashing every moment she'd spent with him wouldn't accomplish anything except to undermine her emotionally.

She was tired, very tired after not having slept the night before, but she wondered if the coming night would be any better. Her eyes were burning, yet she felt unable to close them.

The phone rang. Tessa jumped; then her face closed up, her eyes going curiously blank. "You answer it," she told Silver abruptly. "I'll finishing making the bed."

Frowning, Silver went into the living room and picked up the phone. "Hello." Tessa could hear Silver's side of the conversation clearly from the bedroom, and she tensed. What if it was Brett? No, she was being stupid. Brett wasn't going to call her. He'd gone out of his way to make certain she couldn't reach him by phone, so he wasn't likely to try to call her. Quickly she finished smoothing the comforter, then went into the bathroom and closed the door, running the water so she wouldn't be able to hear anything Silver said.

After a few moments, Silver tapped on the bathroom door, and Tessa hastily shut off the water. "That was your friend Billie."

Tessa opened the door. "Thank you," she said quietly, knowing that no explanations were needed.

Silver thought about passing along everything Billie had told her, but she decided against it. Tessa had already made it clear that she didn't want to discuss Brett Rutland in any way.

Still, it was disquieting that Tessa went immediately to the telephone and unplugged it.

Tessa had a meeting with her lawyer the next day, and Silver went with her. If Calvin Stine didn't approve of having anyone else present, he gave no sign of it. His gray eyes seemed sharper than before as he surveyed Tessa.

"I've talked with John Morrison, the district attorney. He seems to think there's an open-and-shut case against you."

Meeting his eyes, she saw that he didn't believe in her innocence, and her blood chilled. "I didn't take the money," she said, her voice expressionless. "Someone else did."

"Then that someone has done a good job of making it look as if you did it," he pointed out.

"Isn't it your job to find out who that someone is?" Silver broke in, glaring at the man.

He had such cold eyes, Tessa thought. "No, ma'am, that's an investigator's job. My job is to give your niece the best legal counsel and representation in court that I can. My job is to present evidence that contradicts theirs, or to cause the jury to doubt the prosecution's evidence."

"And if the only way of proving my innocence is to find out who is really the guilty one?" Tessa asked softly.

He sighed. "Miss Conway, you've been watching too many 'Perry Mason' reruns. It doesn't work that way. We're dealing with computer theft. There are no marked bills, no fingerprints, no bloody dagger, as it were. Everything is done in an electronic file."

"And my name was used."

"Your name was used," he agreed.

Her back was very straight, her voice as level as his. "Very well, then, where is the money? What have I done with it? Have I spent it? If so, on what? Do you think that an embezzler steals just to stockpile the money somewhere and not use it?"

"It's been known to happen." His eyebrows lifted. "If the money is invested under another name, or simply hidden in a savings account somewhere, an embezzler can expect to serve a fairly short sentence in prison, then collect the money on his or her release and simply disappear."

"So there's no way to prove my innocence unless the real embezzler confesses?"

"That's another unlikely scenario. It doesn't happen."

Tessa got to her feet. "Then I suppose it's up to me," she told him politely. "Thank you for your time."

He got to his feet, frowning slightly. "What do you mean, it's up to you?"

"To prove my innocence, of course."

"How are you going to do that?"

"By tracking down the real embezzler. I know someone who can help."

When they were in the car, Silver said sharply, "Tessa, you don't need him. I think you should hire another lawyer."

"I don't think hiring another lawyer would do any good." Tessa waited for a break in the traffic, then accelerated sharply. "He was being honest with me, and I prefer that to someone who'll only pretend to believe me."

After a moment, Silver nodded. "What are you going to do? Who do you know who can help?"

"I don't know that he will, but I'm going to ask him. His name is Sammy Wallace. He's a genius with computers. If anyone can track down an electronic thief, Sammy can." Then she frowned. "I don't want him to jeopardize his job, though. He works at Carter Engineering, and he'd probably be fired if anyone knew he was trying to help me."

"Ask him anyway," Silver urged. "Let him make his own decision about that. Having to find another job isn't as bad as going to jail!"

For the first time since she'd been arrested, Tessa smiled, really smiled, though it was quickly gone. "No, I guess it isn't." She was faced with prison, something so ghastly that her mind shied away from the thought of it. Suddenly she wondered if she'd be fighting to prove her innocence if she'd only been fired, instead of having charges pressed against her. Would she have accepted the stigma of thief if she didn't have to fight for her freedom as well as her name? She had the shamed feeling that she would have. It would have been the easiest way. But not now. She'd learned the value of honor. Her own sense of honor was all she had left now, that and her freedom, and her freedom was in jeopardy.

Silver bullied her into eating the most substantial meal she'd had since the ordeal had begun; then they cleaned up together and talked about the shop in Gatlinburg, and of the many friends Tessa had in Tennessee. Catching up on the news kept her occupied until the time when she knew Sammy usually got home. He might refuse, of course. Even Sammy had to realize that helping her was a risky business. But all she could do was ask.

She let the phone ring, knowing that if Sammy were tinkering with Nelda, it might take him a while to realize that the phone was ringing. Her patience was rewarded, and on about the twelfth ring he picked up, sounding vaguely surprised as he said, "Hello?" as if his mind were on something else.

"Sammy, this is Tessa."

"Tessa! Where are you? I heard a...well, uh, a rumor, but—"

"It isn't a rumor. I've been arrested for embezzling."

"That's crazy," he said roughly.

"I didn't do it."

"Of course you didn't do it. Did you think you had to tell me?"

"No, of course not," she said gently. "Sammy, I need your help in finding out who really did it. But...it could cost you your job if anyone finds out that you're helping me. So if you don't want to take the risk, I'll understand."

"I'll come over," he said with rare decisiveness. "What's your address?"

She told him, and he hung up. His instant support, like Billie's, made her eyes sting. If only— No! She broke the thought off before it could be fully formed.

It was an hour before Sammy arrived; his blond hair was rumpled, but his normally vague air was missing. He hugged Tessa, cuddling her against his lanky body for a moment. "Don't worry," he said confidently. "I'll find out who did it and get you out of this mess. You want me to use the computers, don't you?"

"Yes, but it isn't going to be easy," she warned.

He grinned, and she could tell that the prospect of matching his wits against the computer excited him. "Tell me what you know."

She didn't really know anything, but she'd gone over and over it in her mind, and settled on the most likely course. A bogus account had been set up in accounts payable, and the computer had been instructed to issue checks to that account. Those checks had then been deposited in a bank, and withdrawals made from the account. But she didn't know the name of the bogus account, and the lack of that extremely important fact made Sammy frown. "I have to have the name, or I don't have a starting place."

Silver said simply, "Ask someone who knows."

Sammy looked startled, then he grinned. "You mean, walk right up to Mr. Rut—"

"No, don't ask him," Tessa interrupted harshly. "It could mean your job. You can't let anyone know you're doing this."

"No one will know. I can do it without tipping anyone off, but I have to have the name. I'll do some snooping around at work." His brow furrowed, then he said, "They had to be using the computers at work to hunt for the bogus account to begin with. They'd have left tracks like anyone else using the computer. If I can't find out something that way, I'll ask around. Someone will know. Maybe Perry will know. After all, you work in his department."

Worked, her mind corrected him. Past tense. Everything was past tense.

The phone rang, and Silver got up to answer it. Panic flaring in her eyes, Tessa hastily asked Sammy, "How is Hillary doing these days?"

"I don't know. I think she's mad at me, but I can't figure out why she should be."

The habit of looking out for Sammy was hard to break. "Pay more attention to her, and see if that doesn't help," she advised.

"Pay attention to her? You mean like taking her out?"

"Well, why not? Would it hurt? You like her, don't you?"

"Yeah, but Hillary doesn't—"

"Hillary does," Tessa assured him, smiling wanly. "She thinks the sun rises and sets on you. Ask her out."

Silver hung up the phone and came back to sit down, her forehead lined with worry. "Trouble on the home front," she sighed. "I left your number at the shop, in case they needed to get in touch with me."

"What's wrong?" Tessa asked.

"A little of everything, evidently. An order of supplies is late, the roof started leaking during a storm last night and a customer who bought a doll for her granddaughter's birthday left the doll on a chair, and her dog got it and chewed it to pieces. It was a custom-made doll." Silver sighed. "Now she wants another one, by Sunday."

After a moment, Tessa said, "I think you need to go home."

"No, they'll just have to get alone without me. I can't leave you now."

"You can always come back," Tessa pointed out. "Nothing will be happening now until the grand jury is called, and that won't be for another two weeks."

Silver hesitated. Her strong practical streak recognized the truth of what Tessa was saying, yet she was still reluctant to leave Tessa. If Tessa had been angry, if she'd cried or called Brett Rutland every name she could think of, Silver wouldn't have worried, but none of that had happened. It was all locked inside Tessa, concealed behind her quiet face and carefully controlled manner, a seething cauldron of pain, outrage and betrayed love. That man had a lot to answer for.

"I'll be all right," Tessa assured her. "Go. Call now and get a flight for tomorrow. You can come back as soon as you've got everything settled, if you'll feel better doing that. Sammy and Billie are here, you know. I won't be alone."

"No. I'll call or come by every day," Sammy promised.

"Well, all right." Silver gave in. "But I'll call you every night, too."

Which meant that she'd have to start answering the phone again, Tessa realized. Well, what did it matter? Brett wasn't going to call her. It was just that she'd developed this silly fear of answering either the phone or the door. She had to get over that, just as she'd have to get over everything else. But deep down, inside her, there was a small cry of pain, because Brett wasn't going to call.

Chapter Eight

Brett sat bolt upright in bed, sweat streaming from his body, his jaw tight from the effort he'd been making not to yell. Swearing under his breath, he kicked the tangled sheet away from his legs and swung out of bed. His heart was still pounding, and he was breathing as if he'd been running miles. Naked, he paced up and down the too-small confines of the hotel room, running his hand through his already tousled hair.

The dream had been so real, but the real horror of it was that it was likely to come true. Tessa had been convicted, and he'd watched her being led away to prison. She'd been wearing a rough, blue uniform dress of sorts, and she'd been so pale and fragile that he'd been afraid she'd collapse. But she'd walked away from him without looking back, flanked on each side by a burly prison guard, and she'd disappeared into a black tunnel. As she'd gone out of sight, an iron-barred gate had slammed shut and locked, and he'd known that he'd never see her again. That was when he'd woken, his throat aching from the silent roar of protest.

The very image was obscene. In the dark truth of the night, he knew that no matter how much money she'd stolen, that even if she had made a fool of him, he couldn't bear for her to go to prison. Not Tessa, with her flashing smile and twinkling eyes, her slow, liquid drawl, the bright laughter that so effortlessly enchanted. And the hot ecstasy of her body, he thought, closing his eyes as the memory slammed into him with the power of a sledgehammer. Her silky legs clasping his hips. The look of trusting passion in her eyes when he took her. The flirtatious, languid movement of her hips when she walked. The incendiary sweep of her long lashes over eyes that laughed and invited. Everything about her drove him mad, and it was the wine-sweet sort of madness that he knew would linger with him for the rest of his life.

He wanted a drink, but a quick look at the clock told him that it was almost two-thirty in the morning. His mouth twisted wryly. That was definitely a little early...or a little late...to start hitting the bottle. His father would nod his head and smirk and say that he'd always said that a woman could drive a man to drink.

The thought of Tom reminded him that he hadn't been able to take Tessa to meet him, as he'd almost promised her he would do, this weekend. But now it was very early Monday morning, and the weekend was over. It had been a week since he'd had Tessa arrested, a week during which he'd been dying a little more each day from the wound caused by her absence.

His emotions had swung from hurt and pain to raw fury; then the anger had changed to outraged pride, and a determination that she would never have the chance to make a fool of him again. Now, however, pride didn't seem very important beside the fact that he'd lose her forever if he let her go to prison. Her guilt no longer mattered. What mattered was that he have her back in his arms again. He'd coddle her and keep her safe for the rest of her life, and make damned sure that she never got in this kind of mess again.

With that inner realization that nothing else meant as much to him as Tessa, he became aware of a growing sense of peace, an easing of the weight on his shoulders. The action he needed to take was abruptly clear. He never thought that it would be easy, but he knew what had to be done. He'd catch the first flight he could get to San Francisco.

He was able to go back to sleep, but he woke early, eager to get things moving. There was no need to pack. He planned to be back that night, even if he had to drive. He showered and shaved, not noticing in the mirror that his face was set in grim determination. After calling the airlines and getting a seat on a flight leaving at nine-twenty, he called Evan.

"I'm going to see Joshua this morning," he said grimly when Evan answered.

"Has something come up?"

"I'm not letting her go to jail."

Evan sighed. "It's about time. What're you going to tell the old man? He was dead set on making an example of the thief."

"I'll handle it." If Joshua didn't decide to make things difficult, he had a plan all worked out, one that would reimburse Joshua and keep Tessa out of jail. If Joshua wouldn't go along with that, Brett knew what he had to do.

"Have you talked to Tessa?"

"No. I don't want her to know anything about it yet." Perhaps it was a little cruel to keep her in the dark, but not as cruel as getting her hopes up and keeping her nerves strung out until she could hear from him again.

"Maybe this will settle things down at work," Evan grunted.

"Maybe." As he hung up, an unwilling grin touched Brett's hard mouth. Tessa didn't lack for support. Everyone was in an uproar, and he was about as welcome as Typhoid Mary. He expected to get a knife in the back at any time from that little red-headed spitfire, and a couple of times he'd had the uneasy feeling that the papers in his office weren't exactly as he'd left them. It didn't matter, because he kept all important papers locked in his briefcase, and all the evidence against Tessa was in the D.A.'s possession, but if he caught anyone in his office they'd be fired on the spot. Even spineless Perry Smitherman had gotten huffy with him, something that had given him a moment of bitter amusement at the incongruity of it.

Shortly before noon, he was striding through the plush dove-gray carpeted corridors of the Carter-Marshall building. Some of the people he passed greeted him; most didn't. The frown on his face was enough to discourage all but the most intrepid.

He entered Joshua Carter's office, and the secretary looked up. A smile lit her pretty face as she recognized him. "This is a surprise. We weren't expecting you, were we?"

"No, we weren't," he growled, but he managed a tight smile for her. Donna had done a lot of favors for him in the past.

"Are you back for good...until the next crisis, that is?"

"Just a flying visit. I need to see Joshua. It's urgent."

Donna pursed her lips, frowning. "Well, he has a luncheon appointment, but I'll stall them. Go on in."

"Thanks. I'll dance at your next wedding."

"Deliver me," she muttered. Donna was currently off men, having just gotten through a messy divorce.

Brett gave the door one hard rap, then opened it. Joshua Carter looked up from his desk, surprise widening his eyes; then he grinned. "Hell, I should've known who it was from the way you came barging in, but I didn't know you were back. Everything sewn up down there?''

Brett put his briefcase on a chair and walked over to the bar that occupied one end of Joshua's office, going behind it to the coffeepot that was always kept full. He poured a steaming cup of coffee, then looked up at his employer. Joshua was of medium height, but bulky from a lifetime of doing hard manual work. His gray hair was thinning, and he had to wear glasses now, but there was still a glint in his hard blue eyes that warned people he was a formidable opponent. Joshua had started out dirt poor, but by his own crafty intelligence and sheer determination he'd built a fortune. He wouldn't be inclined to dismiss charges against someone who'd been stealing from him. In Brett, he'd met his match in willpower, and now they were going to do some hard dealing.

"Let's negotiate," Brett said evenly.

At the tone of Brett's voice, Joshua lifted one gray eyebrow, his blue eyes growing cautious. "Negotiate? This sounds serious. Is some head-hunter stealing you away?"

"No. It's the case in Los Angeles."

"The woman you caught embezzling? What about her?"

"I want to make a deal with her."

"What sort of deal?" Joshua blazed.

"All charges dropped in exchange for full restitution."

Joshua got to his feet and braced his hands on his desk. He drew a deep breath. "There's no way in hell."

Brett sipped the coffee. That was exactly the response he'd expected. "I don't want her in prison," he said coolly.

If there was anything Joshua was, it was shrewd. He looked at Brett for a long, hard minute before he snorted. "But you do want her in your bed, don't you?"

"Exactly."

"I never thought I'd see the day," Joshua muttered. "I think I need some coffee, too." As the older man crossed the room, Brett poured another cup of coffee and set it on the bar. Joshua sat down on one of the stools and picked up the coffee. "I'm not inclined to let her off with a slap on the wrist. How much is missing? Fifty thousand?"

"Fifty-four."

"What did she take it for? Jewelry? A fancy vacation?"

Brett shrugged. He hadn't seen any evidence that she'd spent the money on anything. She dressed well, but not fifty-four thousand dollars worth. "You'll be paid back."

"She still has the money?"

"I don't know. If she doesn't have it, I'll pay you back."

The gray brows drew together. "Brett, that's an expensive woman you're playing with."

"I'm not playing," Brett said laconically.

"Well, I'll be damned." For the first time, a faintly helpless note entered Joshua's voice. He was genuinely fond of Brett, a man made in his own mold, someone who let nothing interfere with getting the job done...or at least, nothing until this woman. "She must be something."

"She's special. The L.A. office is practically in revolt against me for arresting her. Evan's been dragging around like a whipped hound." Brett pushed his fingers through his tawny hair. "And I'm worse than all of them put together," he admitted raggedly.

"Tell me something. Why should I agree to drop charges against her? Why shouldn't she pay for breaking the law?"

"She has paid." Brett's fingers tightened on the cup of coffee as he remembered her white face. It had been a week since he'd seen her, and he was aching to touch her, to whisper to her that everything was going to be all right, that he'd take care of her.

"You're going to marry her? What if she doesn't want to marry you? I don't imagine you're her favorite person, right now," Joshua pointed out.

Brett knew that, but he hadn't let himself think about it. He'd handle that when the time came, after she was no longer in danger of losing her freedom. When he had the charges against her dropped, when she was safe, then he'd deal with her anger. He still had his own anger to work out, and it would probably be a stormy few days before they got everything settled between them, but he wasn't going to let her slip away from him.

"She'll marry me," he said grimly. Then he looked at Joshua, his navy eyes piercing. He might be cutting his own throat by telling Joshua what he was about to say, but he wasn't going to lie to the man. He'd always been aboveboard in his dealings with Joshua, and he wasn't going to change now. "No matter what your decision, I want you to know that I'll be quitting soon. I'm going back to the ranch...and I want to take Tessa with me."

"That's not a smart thing to tell me," Joshua snapped.

"It was honest," Brett snapped back. He'd never toadied to Joshua, which was one of the reasons Joshua prized him. No matter how black the situation or unpleasant the news, he'd always gotten the truth from Brett.

"This woman...Tessa...is she the reason you're quitting?"

"She's only half of it. I've been getting restless, wanting to go back to the ranch. Ranching is what I do best, what I'm most content doing."

"You're damned good at what you're doing now."

"I'm damned good at ranching, too."

Joshua rubbed his jaw, eyeing Brett. He was shrewd enough to realize that the only thing he could do now was make a deal with Brett, which was exactly what Brett had intended all along. He could either deal, or lose Brett entirely. "Why should I drop those charges, when I'll be losing you either way?"

Brett's eyes gleamed. "Negotiate," he said.

Joshua burst out laughing. "Negotiate, hell! You've been herding me to the exact point you've wanted me at from the minute you walked into this office. I can either cooperate with you, or you're quitting completely, whereas if I drop charges against your woman, your...special consultation services...will be available to me—how often?"

"We can work something out," Brett said smoothly.

Sighing, Joshua held out his hand. "Deal," he said, and Brett shook his hand, while relief unknotted the coil of tension in his belly.

The phone rang, and Tessa paused only fractionally before she turned off the television, which she'd been staring at without realizing what she was watching, and rose to answer the phone. Over the past several days she'd answered calls from Silver and Sammy, while Billie usually came over instead of calling, but still she couldn't stop the shiver that ran down her spine each time she heard a bell peal. Sammy hadn't had any luck, either in finding the account name or any other sort of information that would aid him in a computer search. They were at a dead end, and time was running short on her. The grand jury would meet next week.

The insistent ring reminded her of the phone, and she shook herself to dispel the cold mantle of dread that had settled on her shoulders. She lifted the receiver, expecting to hear Silver's voice again. It was almost ten o'clock in Tennessee, and Silver would be getting ready for bed, but she always called Tessa before turning in for the night.

"Hello."

"Tessa. This is Brett."

She jumped as if she'd been strung, and jerked the receiver away from her ear. She hadn't needed him to tell her who he was. She'd never forget that voice, so low and raspy. Whimpering, gasping for breath, she slammed the receiver onto the cradle before she could hear anything else. Oh, God, oh, God, why had he called now? She'd had everything under control, she hadn't broken down once, but the simple sound of his voice had shattered her fragile defenses. A high, keening sound assaulted her ears as her knees stiffened, then gave way beneath her. Curling into a tight little ball on the floor, Tessa began to weep. The phone was ringing again, but there was no way she could have answered it, even if she had dared.

All the pain of betrayal, of love offered and scorned, burst out of her in great, tearing sobs that shook her entire body and felt as if they were rupturing her chest, shredding her throat. She would have screamed with the pain of it if she'd been able to draw enough breath, but all she could do was huddle on the floor.

She cried until she thought she couldn't cry any more, until her throat was raw and burning, the tissues swollen from strain, but still the tears ran down her face. At last she managed to stumble to her feet, and she made her way to the bathroom, bent over like someone old, her hand against the wall for support. There she splashed cold water on her face, gasping at the shock of it, but the sudden coldness gave her back a measure of control. She hung over the sink, shuddering with the effort she was making to stop crying, but at last she managed it and slowly straightened. Her reflection in the mirror made her gasp again; her face was red and splotchy, her eyes swollen almost together from the violent siege of weeping that she'd endured. Staring at her face, at the haunted emptiness of her eyes, she wondered if she'd ever be able to forget about him, if she'd ever stop feeling the pain of knowing that he'd never loved her at all.

She drank some water, and almost choked as the liquid ran down her raw, abused throat. Why had he called? To gloat? Hadn't he beaten her down enough?

The telephone was ringing again. Desperately Tessa ran into the living room and unplugged it, but the sudden silence was almost as unnerving as the noise had been. She chewed her lip. Perhaps that had been Silver, or Sammy, but it didn't matter. She simply couldn't take the chance that Brett might be calling again. She couldn't bear it; she just couldn't take any more.

That night too was sleepless, and endless. The strain of it was in her face the next morning. The swelling had subsided, but she was colorless, and dark shadows lay under her eyes. The first thing she had to do was call Silver and reassure her that everything was all right, even though Tessa felt as if nothing would ever be right again. She plugged in the telephone and punched in the numbers, but when Silver answered the phone on the first ring, as if she'd been waiting anxiously, Tessa found that she couldn't say anything.

"Hello? Hello?" Silver said frantically.

With an effort, Tessa cleared her throat, wincing at the raw pain. "Aunt Silver," she croaked.

"Tessa? Is that you? What's wrong?"

Once again Tessa tried to speak, but no sound came out. Swallowing again, she managed, "Sore throat."

"Oh, my goodness, honey, I guess so! Have you been to a doctor? There wasn't any answer last night, and I've been going out of my mind with worry. When did you get sick?"

"Last night." Each word came a little easier, but her voice was totally alien to her, as hoarse as a frog's and only a little more intelligible. It would only worry Silver to tell her what had happened, so Tessa let her think that she'd come down with something that affected her throat. As a child she'd been prone to sore throats and bouts of laryngitis anyway, so Silver wouldn't think this was unusual.

"Well, take care of yourself, hear? I won't call you while you can't talk, honey, so you call me when you're better. And if you haven't been to a doctor, go to one today. Promise me, now."

Tessa croaked a sound that Silver took for a promise. They hung up, and she promptly unplugged the telephone again. At this rate, she was going to wear the little plastic plug out within a month. If it really mattered, she thought, stricken by the realization that unless Sammy could work a miracle, she wouldn't be needing a telephone for a long time. She should probably have it taken out anyway, to save as much money as she could.

Forcing herself to move, she showered and washed her hair, lingering in the steamy warmth in an effort to soothe her throat until the hot water began to go. Too listless to fool with her hair, she simply towel-dried it and combed it out, to let it finish drying in a straight mass on her shoulders. When she was dressed she poured orange juice over ice and drank that for her breakfast, hoping that the cold would alleviate the swelling in her throat, since the steam in the bathroom hadn't helped any.

It was late in the morning when someone rang her doorbell, then began pounding on the door. Tessa froze, tears stinging her eyes again. There was no way she was going to answer that door.

"Miss Conway! Are you in there? This is Calvin Stine. I need to talk to you immediately."

Her brow knit. Why did he sound so urgent? What had happened? Did this have something to do with Brett calling the night before? She hurried to the door, fumbling with the lock and the safety chain until she could remove them and swing the door open. Calvin Stine stepped inside, smartly dressed in a dark blue suit, his dark brows lowered over his cool, piercing gray eyes.

She closed the door and faced him, her hands clasped together in front of her, her pale face anxious. Her eyes questioned him.

"Please get dressed, as swiftly as you can," he instructed. "I've been trying to call you all morning, but your phone is evidently out of order. The assistant district attorney has called us to a meeting in his office in an hour and a half."

She stood very still, feeling like a small, hunted animal. "Please hurry," he said irritably. "The traffic is a mess this morning. It'll take us at least an hour to get there. By the way, have you reported your phone?"

Tessa shook her head, and moved slowly over to the telephone. Lifting the cord, she showed him that it was unplugged. If he'd been irritated before, he was downright aggravated now.

"That wasn't very smart, Miss Conway. It would've saved me a trip over here if I could have talked to you on the phone."

Silently she went into her bedroom and closed the door. She dressed mechanically in a white linen suit with a pencil slim skirt and a short, smart jacket. Perhaps white wasn't the wisest choice, given her own pallor, but she didn't feel capable of the extra effort that changing would require. After slapping on her makeup, she viewed the garish effort in the mirror and seized a tissue to wipe most of it off. She was too pale to look like anything other than a painted clown if she wore the full routine. Her hair was still damp, and lack of time prevented her from doing anything to it, so she twisted it into a knot and pinned it on top of her head. Twenty minutes after she'd walked into the bedroom, she walked out again, her face expressionless, her purse tucked under her arm. No matter what was going on, she wasn't going to break down again. She wouldn't give them the satisfaction. At that point in her thoughts, "them" was everyone except Silver, Billie and Sammy, and that included her own lawyer.

He checked his watch. "That was certainly fast." Then he looked critically at her pale, frozen face. "Don't be so frightened. This is just a meeting."

She nodded slowly, and abruptly he realized that she hadn't spoken a word since he'd entered the apartment. He frowned again. "Miss Conway, are you all right?"

"Yes," she said, forcing out the strained, stifled word. "I'm perfectly all right."

"Are you ill?"

"No." She walked past him. "Shall I drive my car, too, to save you a trip back here?"

He winced at her harsh, barely audible voice. "No, we could be separated in the traffic. Have you taken anything for your throat?"

Why was he so concerned about her throat? She didn't bother to answer, and he followed her out of the apartment, locking the door behind him. He took her elbow, his fingers oddly gentle as he walked her to his car and opened the door for her.

"The assistant district attorney is Owen McCary," he told her during the drive. "I'm optimistic about this meeting. I think they're going to offer to accept a plea-bargain. It's entirely possible that a trial won't be necessary, that you'll be given a suspended sentence and placed on probation."

Was that supposed to thrill her? Tessa looked out the window, feeling cold and distant, a little disoriented. She completely missed the reluctantly worried way that Calvin Stine looked at her, the puzzlement in his eyes.

The traffic was a snarled mess, just as he'd said, but they made it with about five minutes to spare. It took those five minutes to make their way to the district attorney's office, where a pleasant young man took them to a small, private office. As soon as Calvin ushered her into the office with his hand on the small of her back, Tessa saw Brett's dark, controlled face, and her mind mercifully went blank. She was unaware of being seated, or of the reassuring pat that Calvin gave her cold hand.

The wonderful, protective blankness didn't last long. Voices intruded on her consciousness as people were introduced, and she looked slowly around the office in an effort to orient herself, but she was very careful not to look at Brett. Evan Brady was there, of course, his nervous energy practically throwing off sparks. Owen McCary, the assistant district attorney, sat at his desk looking for all the world like the stereotypical California golden blond, except for the weary street wisdom in his eyes. There was another man, a tall, silver-haired man, and he was introduced as Benjamin Stiefel, an attorney for Carter-Marshall.

She could feel the searing power of Brett's eyes on her, feel him willing her to look at him, and she withdrew even deeper into herself. She locked herself away in her mind, sheltering herself in thoughts that took her away from the meeting. Let Calvin handle it. That was what she'd hired him for.

From the moment she'd walked into the room, he'd found breathing difficult, almost impossible. She was so pale, her face so still, and she looked even more fragile than he'd remembered. The wide, mobile, exotic bloom of her mouth was quiet. There was no lovely, enticing smile curling her lips now, though of course he hadn't expected smiles, not yet, anyway. But he had expected her to use her formidable charm, the disarming, enchanting play of lashes over luminous eyes, and instead she sat like a delicate marble statue, never looking at him, even though he willed her to with fierce concentration. He wanted her eyes to meet his. He wanted to reassure her that everything was going to be all right.

She'd hung up on him the night before, and though he'd wanted to shake her for it, he felt that he understood how she felt. She hadn't known then that he was offering her her freedom.

What was she thinking? Her face had always been so expressive, so alive, but now it was as if she wore a mask. Why wouldn't she look at him? When she heard the offer, would she cry? He couldn't stand the idea of her crying, even in relief. He'd take her out of here, to a place where they could be alone together; then he'd dry her tears, and begin the process of cementing their relationship.

If only she'd look at him.

"Miss Conway. Tessa," Calvin Stine said gently, drawing her attention to him. She regarded him somberly, waiting for him to tell her why he'd drawn her from the cocoon of her thoughts.

He took her hand, enfolding it in both of his as if to warm her cold fingers. "Mr. Rutland has proposed, with the approval of the district attorney's office, that the charges against you be dismissed if you agree to sign a statement of guilt, and to repay the money that is missing." He spoke softly, so softly that only she could hear him. The others in the room must think they were conferring, rather than that he was explaining some-thing she should have been listening to herself. But Calvin's gray eyes gentled as they moved over her face. "Tessa, do you understand?"

"Yes, I understand," she whispered.

There was a stunned, haunted expression in her eyes, and instinctively he moved in front of her, shielding her from the view of everyone else in the room. "I advise you to accept their offer," he murmured urgently. "You've been through enough. I can't tell you how risky a trial would be."

Her stifled voice was barely audible. "You don't think I have a chance of acquittal?"

"Only a slim one, I'm afraid. Their evidence is very strong. Don't take the chance. You couldn't survive in prison," he said angrily.

Why was he so angry? He didn't believe in her in-nocence, hadn't from the beginning. But in the view of the law, even the guilty were entitled to competent le-gal representation, and that was what he was offering now. He was attempting to give her the best advice he could.

A little sigh escaped her as weariness pulled at her limbs. "I'd have to sign an admission of guilt? A confession?"

"That's what they want, yes."

She smiled now, a slow movement of her pale lips. "But I'm not guilty."

A desperate look came into his eyes. "Don't even think it, Tessa. Take the chance they're offering you and run with it."

"I'd have to run. I certainly couldn't face myself in the mirror in the mornings. My self-respect, my good name, are all I have left, and I wouldn't have those if I signed a confession that isn't true. It would be an act of cowardice." Her voice broke several times, and the sounds were harsh and strained, but she managed to say what she felt.

"My God, this isn't the time for nobility!"

"Oh, I'm not noble at all. I'm desperate." She turned her hand in his until *she* was holding *him*, trying to make him understand. "I won't do it. I'm sorry, but I can't admit to something I didn't do."

He bit off the curses that rose to his lips. He was pale, too, and sweating. Behind him, the others were shifting restlessly, wondering about the extended conference, the pleading note they had detected in Calvin's hushed voice. Tessa released Calvin's hands and stood up, her eyes on Owen McCary. She didn't dare look anywhere else.

"I refuse to accept the offer," she said, straining her voice to achieve the necessary volume. "I won't admit to something I didn't do."

Brett surged to his feet, uttering a violent oath. Tessa didn't look at him, but she sensed that he moved toward her, and her heart stopped beating. Clinging tightly to Calvin's arm, she walked past Brett as if he were invisible.

The door closed behind them, and in the pool of silence that was left behind, Evan swore shakily. Brett turned to face him, his eyes burning with an emotion that couldn't be named. A feeling of horror was clawing at his insides. "God in heaven, what have I done to her?" he choked. "She's innocent. *She didn't do it!*"

Benjamin Stiefel sighed. "I never expected this."

That was an understatement, Brett thought savagely. Like a wild animal he turned on Owen McCary. "Drop the charges. Completely. Now." He bit the words off like bullets.

McCary was shaken, too, but he said, "Mr. Rutland, the evidence against her is very strong—"

"I know how strong it is," Brett interrupted harshly. "I'm the one who found it. But I didn't look far enough. I didn't find out who set this up to make Tessa take the blame for it. *I'm dropping the charges*, as of right now."

Benjamin Stiefel tried to interject a bit of caution. "Brett, I don't think Mr. Carter will approve—"

"I'm not asking for his approval. I have the authority to withdraw the charges, and I'm doing it. He'll have his thief, all right. I'll bring him to Joshua Carter on a silver platter."

Evan's dark eyes were full of the same anger that burned in Brett. "Ben, we nearly sent an innocent woman to prison. It didn't seem right from the beginning. It just didn't fit in with the type of person she is. We'll keep Mr. Carter posted on what we're doing, and if he doesn't like it''—Evan shrugged his shoulders—''let him fire us.''

Brett paced the office like a caged animal, his control shattered by the events that had just taken place. Without thinking it out in a logical progression, he'd known as soon as she'd refused his offer that she was innocent. He'd known it instinctively, and without doubt. He'd driven her to the very edge, hurt her—he winced at the thought of how he must have hurt her. No wonder she wouldn't look at him!

He'd give anything to turn back time, to wipe this past week out of existence for her. Every protective male instinct in him was aroused, and outraged, because he'd almost destroyed the very person he loved most in the world. He had to find the real embezzler now, to clear Tessa's name in everyone's mind as well as on paper. It was the only reparation he could offer her.

Chapter Nine

Calvin didn't want to leave her. He took her back to the apartment, but seemed totally incapable of walking away from her. She sat on the couch and watched him as he prowled restlessly around, wondering what he wanted. He kept watching her, too, with a stricken look in his gray eyes, as if he still couldn't believe what she'd done.

Finally his pacing began to wear on her nerves, even through the remote emotional exile she'd placed herself in. "Calvin, I'm sorry," she croaked in as soft a voice as she could manage. "I know you advised me to do the most sensible thing."

"It isn't that." His voice was muffled. "It's just...ah, hell, I've forgotten what it is like to trust someone, to simply be able to take their word on something. I should've trusted you, but I didn't. I was so damned cynical that I thought your guilt or innocence didn't matter to me as a lawyer.''

"It doesn't. It can't, or you wouldn't be able to do your job." Why was she trying to comfort him? She was so tired, and she wanted to go to sleep. If he would just leave, she could wrap herself up in a blanket and lie on the couch. She felt as if she wouldn't be able to keep going much longer. Her legs and arms were leaden, and fatigue dragged at her.

Someone beat on the door, and it sounded as if they were using their fist. Calvin looked at her, but Tessa made no move to get up and answer it. She'd gone very still, like a small animal when a hawk flies over, so he answered the door himself. Brett Rutland filled the doorway, his face dark and dangerous, his eyes savage. "How is she?" he barked.

Calvin turned and looked at Tessa, but she stared straight ahead, not looking in their direction. Brett shouldered past him, ignoring Calvin's sharp, "Mr. Rutland, this is highly irregular—"

"I don't give a damn about irregular," Brett snapped, crossing to Tessa and hunkering down in front of her so he could see her face. Her eyes slid away from him to focus blindly on some spot on the wall. He reached out and took her hand, and that small touch electrified him. It had been so long since he'd felt her skin, been close enough to smell her subtle fragrance. He wanted to lift her in his arms and hug her to him, but she was so pale and stiff, withdrawing from him without actually moving. Her hands were icy. He captured her other hand and held both of them in his in an effort to warm them.

"Tessa, I've dropped the charges. Do you understand? You're clear. You don't have to be afraid."

Calvin was galvanized into speech. "What? You've dropped the charges? But why—I don't understand."

"I'll explain it all to you in a minute," Brett said without taking his eyes from Tessa's face. "Tessa, do you understand what I'm telling you?"

"Yes," she whispered, too numb to feel anything, not relief, or surprise, or even curiosity. She didn't want to feel; she didn't want to think. Not now, with Brett so close. Why didn't he go away? Why didn't he let go of her hands?

"What's wrong with your voice?" he asked sharply.

She looked at him then, and he drew in a convulsive breath at the look in her eyes. "Go away."

Something in her eyes, her face, convinced him to let her go. He released her hands and got to his feet, his bronzed features set. "Let's talk in the kitchen," he said to Calvin, and the two men left the room. Tessa remained where she was, alarmed that they were discussing her, but totally unable to go in there when Brett was there. His presence overwhelmed her, brought too much pain for her to handle, for her even to cope with in any way except to admit to its existence. She couldn't examine it; she couldn't face it.

It seemed as if time dragged, that they spent hours in the kitchen. She wanted desperately to lie down and sleep, but she didn't dare, not with Brett so close. What could they be talking about? Surely there weren't any legal difficulties involved in dropping charges against someone? The charges had really been dropped, he'd said. She was free. She no longer had the grim specter of prison hanging over her head. Why didn't it seem real to her?

When they came out of the kitchen, Calvin crossed over to her and clasped her hand. "You'll be okay," he reassured her. "Mr. Rutland is going to take care of everything. I have to get back to the office, but I'll be in touch with you later."

"Wait," Tessa whispered desperately, her eyes darting to Brett. He wasn't going to leave her alone with Brett, was he?

"Mr. Rutland will take care of everything," Calvin repeated; then he dropped her hand and went to the door. Tessa struggled to her feet. She had to stop him; she had to do something. She couldn't stay there with Brett! But Brett moved, his broad shoulders blocking her as he went with Calvin to the door, and Tessa hesitated, not willing to go so close to him. He closed the door behind Calvin, and turned to face her.

Desperation gave her strength. She swallowed, causing her throat to tighten in pain, but she looked straight at him and said hoarsely, "Get out of my apartment."

"What's wrong with your voice?" he asked again, ignoring her order. Before she could evade him, he'd crossed to stand very close to her, and for the first time she noticed that he held a glass in his hand, a glass of clear, yellowish liquid. He put the glass in her hand, wrapping her fingers around it, and it was so hot that she almost couldn't hold it.

"Hot lemonade," he said. "Drink it. It'll be good for your throat."

It felt like heaven to her cold fingers, and because it was a remedy that she'd often been treated with as a child, she raised the glass to her lips and cautiously sipped the hot, tangy mixture of sweet and sour. The taste was a sweet memory on her tongue, and burned on her throat, but it felt good for all of that.

"What's wrong with your voice? Are you sick?"

Why couldn't he just leave her alone? He was going to badger her with the same question over and over until she screamed, or went mad, or both. "No, I'm not sick!" she yelled, but it came out as only a stifled rasp.

"Then what's wrong?"

His persistence ate at her, destroying her control, but then, he was the only man who'd ever been able to make her react in ways she couldn't control. She drew away from him, a fine trembling beginning to shake her body as she stared at him, at the hard, unhandsome face and the stunning blue beauty of his eyes, the same face and eyes that had held her bemused from the first time she'd seen him. She'd loved him, and he'd turned on her. The trembling grew worse, and suddenly she erupted into rage, her face twisting as she hurled the contents of the glass at him. "Damn you! I hate you! I hate you, do you hear?"

The night before, the sound of his voice had shattered the barriers that she'd built around the hurt she felt, and now he'd broken the control she'd had on the seething anger that had been building up inside her. She flew at him, her fists beating at his face, his chest, any part of him that she could reach, screaming wildly in her stifled voice, but the stress on her throat was too much and her voice began to go entirely, until the screams were silent. Tears streamed from her eyes as the hysteria built in her. Brett jerked his head back, protecting his face, but he simply stood there and let her pound at his chest, absorbing the blows and the pain, the rage, his own heart aching at what he'd done to her. When her strength was gone, she sagged weakly against him, and only then did he put his arms around her, stilling her feebly pounding hands.

"Baby, I'd let you throw boiling water at me if it would make you feel better," he said raggedly, brushing his lips against her hair, her forehead, her temples. "God, if I could only undo it all!" It was a bitter cry from the depths of his soul.

The feel of his arms around her was so painful that she almost couldn't bear it, yet she didn't feel able to push him away. His shirt and suit jacket were sticky from the lemonade that she'd thrown on him, and it was making her face and hair sticky, too, yet her head lay tiredly on the broad expanse of his chest. The lemonade wouldn't ruin the expensive wool, she thought fuzzily, but she was glad that he'd have the expense of having it cleaned.

The room swung around her in a dizzy arc as he lifted her in his arms and carried her into the kitchen, where he sat her on a chair. He wetted a paper towel and washed the stickiness from her face, then dabbed at her hair. Gently he removed the pins from the knot on top of her head and raked his fingers through her hair, tumbling the dark mass down around her shoulders. Then he poured another glass of lemonade for her, and pressed it into her hand. "Here's the rest of the lemonade. Throw it at me if you want, but it'll do you more good if you drink it."

Obediently she drank it, too exhausted and empty to do otherwise, watching him as he took off his coat and tossed it over the back of a chair, then unbuttoned his shirt and took it off, too. The sight of his naked, powerful torso made the bottom drop out of her stomach. She had curled her fingers in the dark hair that covered his broad chest, had noted that it was several shades darker than the tawny, sun-streaked brown of the hair on his head. The memory of the way his body had felt under her lightly stroking, exploring fingers made her jerk her eyes away from him to stare blindly at the floor as he washed the lemonade from his chest and shoulders, but she saw in her mind's eye the way the muscles in her arms and back would flex as he moved, his biceps bulging, rippling.

"Come on, finish that," he said gently, and she jumped, because she hadn't realized he'd moved to her side. He was rubbing a towel over his torso, but his attention was on her. She drank the rest of the lemonade, then handed him the empty glass. He rinsed it out and placed it in the dish drainer to dry, then came back to her and bent down, one arm sliding under her knees and the other going around her back. He lifted her, and Tessa made a hoarse sound of protest.

"Shhh," he soothed. "Don't try to talk; you'll only hurt your throat. You're exhausted, and you need to sleep. I'm just going to put you to bed. When you wake up, you'll feel better, and then we'll talk."

He carried her into the bedroom, and panic made her twist in his arms, but all her strength was gone, and he undressed her as easily as he would have a fractious child. When she was naked, he placed her between the cool sheets, then crossed to the window and pulled the shade down, shutting out the bright California sun. She lay frozen, unwilling to get up while he was there, exposing herself to him again, and equally unwilling to lie in that bed. He removed his shoes and socks, then undid his pants and dropped them.

Tessa struggled upright, a silent protest on her lips. "No, don't try to talk," he said sternly, stepping out of his briefs and coming to her totally, gloriously naked. He got into bed with her and forced her back against the pillows. "Just sleep, baby. I'm going to hold you, that's all. I said no talking," he repeated as she tried again to say something. "You've strained your throat, and you're going to have to let it rest." He drew her against him, his nakedness searing her like a furnace, the warmth enveloping her and sinking into her. His arms were living bonds, wrapped around her, and the hollow of his shoulder made a resting place for her head. The urgent thrust of his masculinity made her struggle weakly for a moment, but he made no sexual advances to her, merely held her, and she was so tired that her brief struggles ceased.

"Go to sleep, darling," he whispered, and she did.

Hours later, she woke to total darkness and an urgent need for the bathroom. She fought out of the grasp of his arms and the tangle of the sheets to stumble, still half-asleep, to the bathroom. When she came out he was leaning against the wall in the hallway, waiting. Without a word he took her back to bed and once again settled her in his arms. Tessa burrowed her face against the warm strength of his neck, inhaling the unforgotten, faintly musky scent of his skin, and fell deeply asleep again, the long periods of unconsciousness just what she needed for both body and spirit.

When she woke again, she was alone in the bed, and an inborn sensitivity to the sun and the passage of time told her that it was late in the afternoon, which meant that she'd slept more than twenty-four hours, at least. She felt dopey from sleep, yet stronger than she had in what seemed like an eternity. Was Brett still in the apartment? Oddly, she wasn't alarmed by the possibility that he might be. Well rested, she was capable of facing him now. Getting out of bed, she wrapped herself in a robe, then gathered her clothes and went to the bathroom. A shower was the most urgent thing on her agenda, and she took a long one, letting the briskly cool water finish washing away the cobwebs in her mind.

The little grooming rituals of brushing her teeth and combing her hair were soothing, and made her feel even better than she had before. Finding Brett waiting patiently outside the bathroom door made her entire body quiver in reaction, but the panic was gone now.

"Breakfast is ready," he announced, then smiled faintly, but the smile wasn't reflected in his eyes. "I guess it's still breakfast, even though it is almost four in the afternoon. I figured you had to like oatmeal, otherwise you wouldn't have bought it, and that'll be easiest on your throat. How is your throat? Can you talk?"

"Yes," she said, a little embarrassed at her froglike croak.

His hard, warm hand went to her wrist, and before she could draw away he had bent down and kissed her mouth briefly. "Don't worry, your voice will come back," he comforted, gently urging her toward the kitchen with the pressure of his hand.

She was so rattled by the touch of his mouth on hers that her hands were shaking as she ate her hot oatmeal, which he must have prepared as soon as he heard her stirring. Why had he kissed her? For that matter, why had be bothered to spend the night with her? Certainly not because of love, she thought tiredly. Guilt, probably. Well, that was his cross to bear, because she had her own problems, not the least of which was getting over him. If she ever could. If she'd ever see another day when she didn't think about him, ever wake up in the morning and not wish that he was beside her. Somehow, she just didn't think that day would ever come.

He was wearing different clothes, she noticed, khaki pants and a pullover white cotton shirt that fit loosely, with the sleeves rolled up over his brawny forearms. "When did you go back to the hotel?" she asked hoarsely, indicating the clothes.

"I didn't. I called Evan, and he brought my clothes over. I didn't want to leave you, even for an hour."

She sipped her coffee thoughtfully, and it was a moment before she spoke. "I'm all right. I'm not going to do something stupid, if that's what you're thinking."

"No, that wasn't what I was thinking. I was afraid that you'd wake up while I was gone, and lock me out," he said simply.

She nodded. "Yes," she said.

"I couldn't take that chance. Not now." His voice roughened. "I know I can't make it up to you for what you've been through this past week, but I swear I'm going to spend the rest of my life trying."

Anger stirred in her. "I don't need your guilt! I told you, I'm all right."

He drank his own coffee, not responding to her heated statement. "I called your aunt," he said instead, totally surprising her. "I found her number in your telephone index. By the way, you have it listed under A, instead of S."

"It's Aunt Silver, not Silver Aunt," Tessa muttered distractedly. "Why did you call her?"

"I knew she had to be worried about you, and I wanted her to know that it's over with, at least as far as you're concerned. I still have a thief to catch," he added grimly.

Again, Tessa was startled. "What do you mean?"

"I know you didn't do it."

"You do? What about all of that famous evidence?" she rasped, rising to her feet in agitation.

"I was wrong. You didn't do it."

The steadiness of his gaze had the opposite effect on her; it shook her instead of calming her. She hadn't really thought about the whys and wherefores of it, hadn't wondered about his reason for dropping the charges. She had assumed simply that he felt sorry for her, or perhaps was having an attack of conscience over the fact that he'd seduced her for the purpose of his investigation. To hear him state flatly that he thought she was innocent was almost more than she could take in.

"I don't understand," she said shakily. "Why should you believe me now, when you didn't before? The evidence hasn't changed, has it? Have you learned something else?"

"No. Nothing new had turned up." It would take too long to explain his feelings to her, and she wasn't ready to hear about them anyway. He'd lain awake for hours the night before, holding her in his arms while she slept, examining his sudden strong conviction that he'd wrongly accused her. Part of it had been the staggering realization of her unyielding sense of honor, so strong that she wouldn't betray it even to protect herself. But even more, it had been the way she had loved, the open, unreserved way she'd given herself, and her virginity, to him. She was twenty-five, and she'd been engaged twice before. He certainly hadn't expected her to be a virgin. No one would have. Yet she'd remained a virgin out of a deep sense of self-respect, an inner knowledge that perhaps she wasn't ready yet to commit herself to that sort of intimacy with a man. She hadn't loved her fiancé enough to forgive him his infidelity, and neither had she loved him enough to give him herself.

He felt tension coiling in his gut. Would she love him enough to forgive him? She'd loved him enough to give him the sweetness of her body, but that had been before he'd taken her love and trampled on it. What would he do if she couldn't forgive him?

Tessa stood uncertainly by her chair, the expression on his face making her shy away from the subject. Instead she went back to the previous topic. "What did Aunt Silver say?"

"She cried," Brett said abruptly. She'd also said some things to him that had scorched the telephone lines, but they were between him and Silver only. He'd deserved most of the things she'd said. It wasn't until she had accused him of using Tessa that he'd brought her up short. Silver, at least, now knew exactly what his intentions were concerning Tessa. Convincing Tessa, however, was something else, and he knew he'd have to be patient. Only time would heal the wound he'd dealt her. She wouldn't even listen to him right now if he tried to tell her that he loved her.

"Is she...is she coming back this weekend?"

"No. There's no need for it."

Her head drooped on her slender neck. "Then I think I'll go home." Even as hoarse as her voice was, there was poignancy in the way she said "home." She longed for the peace and splendor of the mountains, bursting with the fresh green miracle of spring. She could go hiking, touring the park as she had done every year until she'd moved to California, letting the solitude ease her bruised spirit. There was certainly nothing left for her here. She'd left Tennessee in an effort to get over Andrew, and she'd succeeded beyond her wildest dreams. Andrew was nothing but a vague memory now, forever burned out of her heart by the fires Brett had ignited. She wanted to go home.

Brett was stunned by the thought that she might simply pack up and leave, and he couldn't follow her, not now. He was bound to stay in Los Angeles until he found the embezzler, so he'd have to keep Tessa with him. If he let her go now, he was afraid he'd never be able to get her back.

"You can't leave now," he said sharply.

Her green eyes widened in fear. "I can't?"

"I need your help," he said, improvising rapidly.

She was wary now. "Help doing what?"

"Finding out who framed you," he said promptly.

"I don't see how I can help."

"No one knows that the charges against you have been dropped. The embezzler has to be feeling pretty safe, but if you leave, that could tip him off. He could grab the money and run."

"He?" Tessa asked, lifting her brows.

"A figure of speech."

After a minute, she said, "I don't care if you catch him or not."

He got to his feet, too, a little angry. "You don't want to catch the person who almost caused you to go to prison?"

Automatically, she stepped back. "I know I should want a criminal to be caught and punished, but right now I just don't care. All I want to do now is forget about this...all of this. Everything."

Including me, he thought furiously. Too bad, because he wasn't going to let it happen. His navy eyes were narrowed angry slits as he reached out for her, his hands gentle despite his anger. She went stiff at his touch, but didn't fight him as he eased her into his arms, holding her against him while he stroked her hair. "You're worn out, and you've been through a bad time," he murmured. "Poor baby, I'll make it up to you. You don't have to worry about a thing now; I'll take care of you."

"I'm not worn out, and I can take care of myself." His big body, pressed against her, reminded her too vividly of the times when he'd held her beneath him, making love to her with shattering intensity. Her protest was automatic, and she might have saved her breath for all the attention he paid her.

"I've missed holding you," he said huskily, moving his lips against her temple. "You smell so sweet. Tell me something, honey. Are you pregnant? Are you going to have my baby?"

A bolt of pain shot through her. Was that why he'd dropped the charges? Was all his talk about believing in her innocence just that—talk? "No," she almost spat, bracing her hands against his stomach and trying to push him away. "No, I'm not. I found out last week."

He pulled her hands from his stomach and gently forced her arms behind her back, anchoring them there with one big hand. He was aware of disappointment that she wasn't going to have his baby, but he knew that it was for the best. He didn't want her to associate the conception of their first child with anything except pleasure, anything except love. She felt so good in his arms, as if part of him had been missing and was now restored. The feel of her firm, round breasts pushing against him made his body stir with arousal, a condition aggravated by the fact that he'd held her naked in his arms all night long, longing to make love to her but knowing that she was exhausted, that she desperately needed sleep.

Tessa could feel what was happening to him, and her throat tightened in mingled fear and remembered ecstasy. The ecstasy was a part of her now, a memory that would never leave her, and she feared him because she was so terribly vulnerable to him. She loved him, and he had hurt her worse than she'd ever imagined she would be hurt. Because she loved him, he could hurt her again, and she had no defenses against him. "Brett, please," she groaned. "I don't want that to happen. I can't handle it, not now. Please."

"I know," he reassured her harshly. "I know. I'm not going to do anything except hold you. You know I won't force you, don't you?"

"Yes." The word breathed out of her. In that, she did trust him. Physically, he'd never been anything but tender with her.

He relaxed fractionally, but he still held her tightly to him, and gradually she relaxed, too. After all, she'd slept naked in his arms the night before, and he hadn't done anything, so she felt safe standing in the kitchen fully clothed.

The doorbell rang, and she jerked out of his arms, whirling around like a small, startled animal. "Easy," he soothed, frowning at her reaction. "That's probably Evan. I told him to come by late this afternoon and we'd start work."

"Why can't you work in your hotel room?" she demanded, following him into the living room.

"Because I don't have a hotel room," he explained easily, and opened the door to Evan.

Tessa had an alarming feeling that was too certain to be classified as a suspicion. Rather, she *knew*. But their relationship was too tangled and too private for her to pursue the matter with Evan present, which was something Brett had probably been counting on.

Evan greeted her with a friendliness that put her off stride, particularly when Brett rested his arm heavily around her waist and drew her with him to the couch, keeping her by his side as Evan began pulling papers out of his stuffed briefcase. Tessa sat stiffly for a moment, then moved far enough away from Brett that their bodies weren't touching. Did he think she'd fall for his devoted act? That was all it was, an act, and she wasn't fool enough to be taken in twice. At her movement, Brett's head whipped around, and the expression in his eyes was dangerous, but Evan began talking, and Brett had to turn his attention back to the other man.

"I got some interesting information this afternoon," Evan said with controlled excitement. "The handwriting analysis of the signature on the checks."

Brett leaned forward, and Evan passed him the report. Quickly Brett scanned it, his brows knitting in concentration.

"What does it say?" Tessa asked, tilting her head in an effort to read it.

"It says, darling, that the signature on the checks is very similar to yours, but that there are enough differences to make a definite decision impossible. However, the person who wrote those checks is almost certainly a female, and that rules out the one person we've thought all along was the most likely prospect."

She frowned at the easy endearment, but was distracted by his last sentence. "Who did you think it was?"

"Sammy Wallace," Evan said, accepting the report as Brett passed it back to him.

"Impossible," Tessa said immediately.

"We know that now, but he was the most suspicious. According to you, he has a lot of expensive equipment in his apartment, and it had to be paid for in some way.''

So he'd been using her to get information on her friends, too! She clenched her hands as her anger surged. From being numb, she had gone on an emotional roller-coaster, with her moods swinging from one extreme to the other, as if, now that they had broken free of the control she'd placed on them, they were reacting wildly.

"Sammy has been trying to help me," she said, and both of them looked startled. "If he has the name or number of the account that was used, he can trace it back to the original entry, the time of day it was made, I think even to the original terminal that was used. But he couldn't get the account name.''

A black look crossed Brett's harsh features. "Damn it, I knew someone had been going through the papers in my office!''

She blanched at the thought that she might have gotten Sammy fired. That had been the one thing she had wanted to avoid. "He was only trying to help," she pointed out, and refrained from adding that Sammy had believed her from the beginning.

As if on cue, the doorbell rang. This time she didn't jump, though the sound jangled her nerves. Evan quickly began gathering papers up as Brett went to the door.

Sammy and Billie stood in the doorway, gaping at Brett; then Billie shot to Tessa's defense. "What are you doing here? Get out! How dare you badger her like this!"

"Settle down," Brett advised her coolly. "We're not badgering her. We're trying to find out who set her up."

"What do you mean, set her up?" Billie shot back.

"Just what I said. Well, come on in. This is turning out to be quite a party." He opened the door wider, and Evan came into their view.

"What is this?" Billie asked suspiciously.

Brett jerked his head sideways in silent command, and they both came cautiously into the apartment. "To begin with, we dropped the charges against Tessa yesterday."

Sammy's face brightened, but Billie said, "Is that supposed to make everything all right? You think you can just waltz back in here and take up where you left off?"

A flush pinkened Tessa's wan face, and Brett said grimly, "I should be so lucky. No, that isn't what I think. But someone deliberately made it look as if Tessa was embezzling, and I want to know who it was."

"Billie, please," Tessa interjected, intending to ask Billie to halt the hostilities, but she didn't get any further.

"What's wrong with your voice? You sound like a frog."

"She strained her throat," Brett said, then deftly changed the subject. "Wallace, I understand that you can trace the account if you have either the name or the number."

Sammy eyed him cautiously. "That's right."

"How long would it take you?"

When it came to computers, Sammy lost all his shyness. He was a master in the field, and his confidence showed. "That depends. If I used the master computer at work, a couple of nights. Maybe less."

"How about if that's all you work on tomorrow?"

"You mean, on company time?"

"That's exactly what I mean."

"I can give you the data on the original entry tomorrow."

"Do it," Brett said.

"What's the account name?"

"Conway, Inc.," Brett said softly, sensing the way Tessa stiffened. "They used her name, all the way through."

"No wonder you thought she did it!" Billie muttered.

Sammy was frowning. "No, that's wrong. It isn't Conway, is it?"

"There's another account, under the name of Conmay, Inc. Only one letter is different, and that letter is so similar that, with a dot matrix printer and a bad ribbon, which is the common state of affairs, it's almost impossible to distinguish between the two when you're checking down a list."

Hearing how she'd been set up almost made Tessa ill. "Then my name was used to sign the checks written on the account that the company funds were deposited into...." The evidence had been overwhelming, and all of it had pointed to her. It didn't seem like a casual choice, but a deliberate effort to incriminate her specifically.

Brett looked sharply at her. "That's right."

"I'll work with you tomorrow," Evan said to Sammy. "With both of us on it, we can do it in half the time. Who knows, Brett and I may save our jobs yet."

Tessa froze momentarily, then turned and looked at Brett, a look that was long and very level. "Did you have the authority to drop the charges against me?" she asked quietly.

Brett gave Evan a cutting glance. "I have the authority," he drawled, daring Evan to say anything else.

"Then let me put it another way: Did you have the authorization to drop the charges?"

"Not exactly," he said with a wolfish smile. He didn't like her questions, but he wasn't going to lie to her, not now. There was a lot of information he wouldn't volunteer, but if she asked him a direct question, he was going to answer it honestly. "I took the responsibility for the decision."

"But you could be fired?"

"It's possible, but not likely. Mr. Carter and I have an agreement about things like this. When an on-the-spot decision is called for, I make it."

There were a lot of questions Tessa wanted to ask him about that, but not in front of everyone else. She simply added them to her list of things to ask him about when they were alone—and she had no doubt that they would be alone. When the others left, she knew that Brett would be staying.

It wasn't particularly gratifying to find that she was right, but once they were alone again, she turned to face him. She felt far more balanced now than she had in a week, and though she couldn't help feeling grateful to him for taking care of her the day before, when she'd practically been a basket case, it was past time that she faced him. Putting it off wouldn't lessen the hurt.

"Now we talk," she said.

He nodded, a hint of satisfaction in his eyes, as if he'd found it difficult to restrain himself. "Yes, we do. You've managed to evade the question several times, darling, but now you're going to tell me exactly what *is* wrong with your voice," he said very softly.

Their eyes met, and she saw the determination in his. She gave a wry smile. "I cried too much."

Something changed in his face, but before he could speak again, she drew a deep breath and said, "The next question is mine: Where are you staying, now that you've given up your hotel room?"

His eyes moved over her face, and his voice was gentle but implacable when he said, "I'm staying here."

Chapter Ten

Tessa pulled herself up very straight, her gaze unwavering. "I haven't asked you to stay."

"I know," he admitted dryly. "That's why I had to invite myself."

As she stared at him, she realized that he was determined to stay, to wear down her resistance to him. He made her feel hunted, and desperation made her angry. "Damn it, Brett, it's over!"

"Not by a long shot. I'm not giving up, baby. I'm not going to let you go. What we have together is too good to just give up on."

"We never had anything *together*!" she said bitterly. "I had love, while you had your investigation. Now you have your guilt, and I...I just don't want any part of it," she finished in a dull tone.

He flinched at the lash of her words. "Yes, I feel guilty! I should have trusted you, but I didn't. When I saw your signature on those checks, I went crazy, because I thought you'd been using me as a hedge against being prosecuted!"

"What a lovely opinion you have of me!" she flared, her small hands knotting into fists at her sides.

Brett shoved his fingers through his thick hair, groping for an explanation. "I'm a loner, Tessa. I'm not used to trusting anyone, or to letting anyone get close to me. You got so close to me that you knocked me off balance. That's not much of an excuse, but it's the only one I have. I thought you were using me, and it hurt like hell. It hurt so much that I almost vomited. All I could think of was not to let you know that I was hurting. Damn it, I love you!" he said angrily.

Tears stung her eyes. "Sure you do. You love me so much that you never faced me with the evidence. You didn't even give me a chance to defend myself! Do you have any idea what it's like to be arrested, to be booked and fingerprinted, how humiliating it is? I felt dirty! I tried to call you; I kept thinking that if I could just get in touch with you, everything would be all right, that you'd straighten it all out. Can you even begin to imagine how I felt when I learned that *you* had had me arrested?" Her voice became thickened and strained, almost soundless. "You don't know what love is."

He cursed rawly. This was the first time in his life he'd ever told a woman that he loved her, and she didn't believe him! The hell of it was that he could understand her reasoning. She must think that he was motivated by guilt, that he was taking care of her in an effort to assuage that guilt. And there was nothing he could say that would change her mind; there were no words that could ease her pain. Instead of being betrayed, he had betrayed her. By not trusting her, he had lost *her* trust, and he had hurt her so deeply that she might never recover from it. The thought was so unbearable that he rejected it completely; he would do anything in the world for her, except let her walk out of his life. He would do whatever he had to do to convince her that he loved her, to rekindle the love she felt for him. She was his, and if words weren't enough to convince her of that, then he'd have to use more drastic measures.

Watching him with bitter weariness, Tessa saw his face change, saw his eyes narrow with determination, as a subtle shift of expression hardened his features. Abruptly, he looked more dangerous than a crouching panther.

Slowly he reached out and turned off the lamp. A pool of light spilled into the living room from the kitchen, falling across his face and illuminating half of it, while the other half was shadowed. Tessa caught her breath and instinctively moved back a step, but she couldn't look away from him. She was caught, mesmerized by the burning sensuality of his face as he tugged the white cotton shirt out of his pants and slowly pulled it off over his head, then tossed it to the floor. His bronzed skin gleamed darkly, and the hair on his chest made an even darker shadow against his flesh. "If you won't believe me," he said in a rough whisper, "then I'll have to show you."

Tessa took another backward step, her heart leaping high to lodge in her throat, making breathing difficult. Her eyes were huge and haunted as she stared at him. "What...what are you doing?"

He was stalking her with slow, silent movements, his eyes never leaving her face. "You said that you loved me. Were you lying?"

Whatever she had expected, it wasn't to be questioned. The question demanded her attention, and she stared at him, distracted by the anger building in her. "No, I wasn't lying! Did you think I'm a liar as well as a thief?"

He ignored the last part of her response, moving still another step closer to her. "You were engaged twice before, but you didn't make love with either of them, because you didn't really love them. You love *me*, you went to bed with *me*, and you can't forget what we have any more than I can. No matter what, you still love me, don't you?"

"Will a confession make you feel any better?" she asked raggedly, her body stiff with pain. "Yes, I love you, but I won't waste my life on someone who doesn't love me! I went to you; I wanted to tell you that I loved you, that I was innocent, but you never gave me the chance.''

"I was going to pieces on the inside," he rasped. "It nearly drove me crazy, thinking that you'd been using me. Damn it, Tessa, you know how that feels! You thought the same thing about me!"

Her eyes were raw, burning with the hell inside her. "There's a slight difference," she said, flinging the words at him like stones. "I wasn't trying to send you to prison!"

"When I could think straight again, I knew that I couldn't let you go to prison. Damn it, listen to me!" he growled, grabbing her arm as she turned away and pulling her back to face him. "When I called that meeting in the D.A.'s office, I still thought you were guilty, but it didn't matter. What mattered was protecting you. There was no way I was going to let you go to prison.''

Tessa pulled against the strength of his hands, but he held her effortlessly, his long fingers wrapped around her upper arms. "Let me go," she choked, panic rising in her. She felt stifled by his size, his overwhelming masculinity, and her tenuous hold on her control was slipping. Deep inside her, an insidious need was undermining her resolve; even now, she wanted him, needed him. She needed his heat to ward off the arctic cold that surrounded her; she needed his strength, because she had none left. She was tired, defeated, and she couldn't take much more. "Please," she whimpered. "Let me go."

"No. Never." He shook her lightly. "Tell me that you love me."

"Let me go!"

Watching the way her lips trembled, Brett knew she was close to breaking. He had an agonized moment of indecision about the wisdom of pushing her, but it was his last desperate gamble; he had to break down the wall of icy remoteness she'd built between them, or he'd never be able to reach her again.

"You love me," he said roughly, holding her as she tried to jerk away from him. "I love you. Tell me that you love me. I want to hear it. Tell me!"

Tessa was shaking wildly, staring up at him with desperate eyes. Love him? She ached for him. She felt as if she would die without him, but she'd learned, this past week, that a human being could be acutely miserable and still live, still function. She would give almost anything if she could turn back the clock and totally erase this past week. At least then she would still be living in her fool's paradise. She wouldn't know what it was like to feel the laughter die.

"Tell me that you love me," he insisted, shaking her again.

The acid burning of tears in her eyes blurred his image, then the tears overflowed and began to roll slowly down her cheeks. "Why are you doing this to me?" she whispered. "Haven't you hurt me enough?"

He wouldn't let up. "Tell me that you love me."

"I love you," she said, defeated, giving him the words that he wanted, but the words were stones taken from the wall she'd built to protect herself, and the gap permitted all the forbidden emotions to come rushing in, battering at her, tearing her down. A sobbing gasp broke from her throat, signaling the end of her control. Her head dropped forward and she stood docilely in his grasp, her body shuddering with the force of her weeping. There was something different in her tears, an acceptance of the grief and pain that she'd been denying.

A muscle twitched in Brett's jaw, and he felt his own lips tremble for a moment before he controlled them. Slowly he released her arms and slid his hard hands down to curve around her waist. He pulled her against him so she could feel every line of his body.

Her eyes blinded by tears, Tessa was nevertheless aware that his warm, bare chest was there for her to lay her head on; his powerfully muscled legs supported hers, his thighs taut and corded. He was holding her up, offering her his strength when she had none of her own. Yet she was afraid to depend on that strength, and she turned away from him, only to have him catch her and pull her back against him, and this time her head did fall back on his chest. "How can I trust you?" she wept, not noticing the irony that now their situations had been reversed, but he noticed, and winced.

"In time, love. In time," he breathed. "Just don't throw it away. Give me another chance to show you how much I love you." She was weak now, leaning on him, just as he'd wanted her to be. For now she was utterly defenseless, and he moved to fortify his newly gained position. He bent his head to nibble at her ear, then slid his mouth down the exposed arch of her neck, knowing how sensitive her skin was there. She shuddered and pressed herself against him, her hands reaching back to curve around his thighs and pull him forward, as if she could meld them together. He bit off a groan, sliding his palms up to cover both her breasts.

She rolled her head against his shoulder, tears still rolling down her cheeks, because she wanted him so much. She was afraid to believe him, but she couldn't pull away from him. She was so empty and cold and alone, and he was the warmth that would keep her from dying.

He did groan aloud then, turning her in his arms and lifting her against his chest. "Don't cry, darling. Please don't cry," he whispered as he carried her to bed. He had wanted her to break, but he hadn't known it would hurt so much. All he wanted to do now was to make everything right in her world.

She wrapped her arms around his neck and clung, her face buried in the hollow between his face and shoulder. "I only cried once, right after I was arrested," she gasped between sobs. "But now I can't seem to stop. Oh, Brett, I was so scared!"

"I know, darling, I know." His face was tortured as he placed her on the bed and began undressing her. "I don't ever want to make you cry again." It wasn't easy, getting her clothes off while she clung to his neck, but he managed it. He wouldn't have torn her arms loose for anything in the world. Then he struggled out of his pants and kicked them away, and got into bed with her.

He just held her while she cried, and his own eyes burned. She was his woman, a part of him; it hurt him that she hurt.

At last her sobs became little gasps, then ceased altogether, but still he held her and made no effort to make love to her. Tessa lay quietly in his arms, feeling the soft rasp of his hairy legs against her smooth ones, the hardness of his stomach and chest, the corded strength of his arms around her. She felt as if a momentous decision was forcing itself on her, and she wasn't ready for it, but neither did she want to force an irrevocable break between them. She had thought the break was already there, and she had been in agony at losing him, yet now that another chance had been offered to her, she was afraid to take it. What if she were wrong again? She wanted his love, not his guilt, and if she ever found that he'd offered only a pale image instead of the reality of love, it would break her. Yet she couldn't send him away, not now, when she was so empty and only he could fill her, bring her back to life.

They lay together while he slowly stroked one hand up and down her slender back, the soothing movement lulling her into a drowsy sense of contentment. At least in this moment he was hers. He felt her relaxing against his body. "Better now?" he whispered into her hair.

Her hand moved over his chest, her fingers sliding through the hair. "Yes," she said sleepily. She didn't think about what she said next; the words came out of her subconscious, out of an inborn need to reach out to the man she loved. "Brett...make love to me, please."

His entire body was suddenly taut, quivering with need, the electricity of his sensuality banishing her drowsiness. "Are you sure?"

"Yes," she breathed. "I need you so much." She needed to be as close to him as she could get, to reaffirm her life and freedom in the mingling of their bodies. This night wouldn't answer her questions, but it would help to banish the week of nightmares and desolation. She needed him to make her whole again.

Without another word he rolled atop her, parted her legs, and slid deeply into her. She cried out wordlessly, at both the shock of his entry and the fierce pleasure she felt at their joining, at the moment when they ceased to be two separate beings. He comforted her with a rough murmur, drawing her legs up to wrap them around his waist.

Their lovemaking wasn't prompted so much by passion as it was by a need to come together, to give and receive comfort, yet before long Tessa was gasping as his slow movements wrung new heights of ecstasy from her body. His hands stroked and soothed and excited, and his kisses were so deep and hungry that she was unable to breathe, but breathing wasn't important any longer. The only thing that mattered to her was the man she loved, and in that moment she didn't care what happened.

"I love you," he groaned against her throat. "Tessa!" He gasped her name urgently and seized her hips, lifting her up to meet him. She cried out, too, shuddering with the force of her pleasure and accepting his.

There was silence afterward, but she was content. He lay heavily in her arms, his body damp with sweat, and instead of moving away he pushed himself closer against her. He turned his face into the softness of her neck, murmured something unintelligible, and went to sleep. Tessa held him in her arms, staring at the ceiling in the darkness, wondering why she had asked for his lovemaking, wondering if it had solved anything at all, or only made her thoughts more complicated.

His heavy weight bore down on her, pinning her to the bed, but she wouldn't have moved him for anything. She couldn't regret inviting his lovemaking. It had soothed a deep, crippling pain in her heart. She had been left lost and bewildered by his sudden desertion, and his passion had reassured her that he had really wanted her. She could trust his physical need for her, if not his emotional one.

With his actions that day he had offered her a clear choice, though he probably hadn't meant to give her any choice at all. Her lips moved in a small, resigned smile. Brett Rutland was an autocratic, arrogant, dominating male. Any woman who lived with him would have a constant struggle to keep their relationship balanced. She wanted to be that woman. She *could* be that woman, because Brett had given her the opportunity— if she made the choice to live with him.

She could either trust him or not trust him, and she still felt too confused, too emotionally battered, to rely on herself to make the correct decision. The only thing she didn't doubt was her love for him. That was odd, because she had always thought that love had a limit, that there was a point in any relationship where love could die. That had certainly been her experience with both Will and Andrew, and at the time she had been certain she loved them. Yet had she? What she felt for Brett so far surpassed anything she'd felt before that it made her doubt her own emotions, or at least her ability to read them. Life hadn't always been easy for her. As a young child she had had to accept her father's desertion, and not so many years later the death of her mother. But somehow she had skated around the edges of those emotional disasters, preferring to look at the sun instead of the shadows. The ultimate party girl, that was her. She hadn't been malicious, but still she had slipped away from any relationship that could have touched her deeply, that could have made her care.

Until she met Brett. His character was so intense and powerful that he had overwhelmed her frothy defenses, and at the same time she had been challenged on a very, personal, feminine basis by his cool control. Given their particular personalities, it had been inevitable that she would fall in love with him, truly in love for the first time in her life.

He had hurt her more than she had ever thought she would be able to accept from any man, yet it hadn't killed her love for him. She loved him despite everything, and she wouldn't be getting over it.

Welcome to the big time, Tessa, she told herself in aching realization.

A long time later he stirred in her arms and lifted himself higher against her. Tessa felt awareness tighten his muscles, and gently she stroked her palms over his powerful back.

His voice was a low, sleep-roughened rasp of sound, quiet in the darkness that surrounded them. "Have you slept?"

"No," she murmured, her voice still as rough as his. They were a pair, she thought absently. They both sounded like frogs.

Several minutes passed in silence, while his hand moved slowly, exploringly, over her hip and side. "Any regrets?" he finally asked.

"About this? No," she answered slowly.

"What have you been thinking?"

"That I still love you. That I still hurt. That I still don't know what to do."

He sighed. "It isn't easy, is it? Loving. Hell, I didn't even know what it was."

In the quiet, warm darkness, she felt better able to talk to him than she ever had before. There was only his voice, and the warmth of his body, with no outside distraction to break her concentration. She wanted to concentrate on him, to learn everything she could about this man; she knew him physically, but now she needed to know all the little things that would give her the key to his thoughts. "You love your parents, don't you? Your home? There's your horse, your dog, your first grade teacher...."

A low laugh rumbled through him. "No, I never loved my first grade teacher. As for the ranch...I don't know if it's love. The ranch is a part of me. I can't separate myself from it; no matter where I am or what I'm doing, it's there in my head." He paused for a moment, as if considering the matter. "Horses and dogs...I've had my favorites, but I can't say that I've ever loved an animal. My father...yes, I love him. I owe my life to him, and it wasn't easy for him to take care of me."

"Your mother died?" Tessa asked gently.

"I don't know. She gave me away when I was a week old. She may still be alive, but it doesn't much matter. There's no connection between us now, no curiosity, or sense of need. There never has been. Tom is my natural father, but he wasn't married to my mother. He was working in southwest Texas when he met her. She was a rancher's daughter, and he was just a hired hand, a drifter, but she was wild and looking for a way out, trying to kick the traces. They would meet in an old line shack."

Tessa lay spellbound, caught up in the tale he was telling her in a low, slow voice. She felt as if he were finally giving her the key to himself, unlocking a portion of that private part of his mind.

"She got pregnant, of course. I imagine she could have gotten an abortion, if she had wanted to risk the back-alley operations they had then, but she chose to have me. I was probably the ultimate gesture of rebellion. It caused an almighty scandal, but she refused to tell her folks who the father was, refused to go away, refused to hide herself until after I was born. Tom tried to get her to marry him, but she refused that, too. Ranch life was exactly what she was trying to get away from, and that was all he could offer her. It was all he knew."

He was silent then for so long that Tessa feared that he wasn't going to tell her any more. She touched his hair, sliding her fingers through the tousled, tawny silk. "And when you were born?"

"When I was born, she named me, nursed me for a week, then got in touch with Tom and told him to meet her at the line shack. She took me with her to meet him, handed me to him, and walked away. That was the last time he saw or heard from her. She never went back home, just kept on going."

"So your father raised you by himself."

"Yeah. He left Texas that day, too, because he was afraid her parents would take me away from him if they knew she hadn't taken me with her." In the darkness, she could feel his grin against her skin. "Can you imagine a rough ranch hand lugging a week-old baby cross-country, not knowing the first thing about kids? I imagine the wonder is that I survived."

She found herself chuckling. "I feel sorrier for your father than I do for you!"

"Well, we both survived the diaper stage, and he was always there for me. We didn't have anything, but we were together. He worked his way around the country, taking what jobs he could get. I guess I've been fed in more ranch house kitchens that you could count, sort of like a puppy who wandered in. I'd play in the yard and barns, waiting for Tom to come back in at night, until I got old enough to go with him."

"How old was that?"

"Four or five, I guess."

"That's not old enough!"

"It was old enough to stay in a saddle all day long. I can't remember when I couldn't ride. By the time I was six, I was working. I could rope and cut, and though I wasn't strong enough to bulldog, I could still help with the branding and dipping."

"What about school?"

"That's what decided Tom to settle down. I had to go to school, or somebody would eventually notify the authorities and I might have been taken away from him. We were in Wyoming at the time, so he spent every cent he had on a piece of land, built a shack for us to live in, and started ranching for himself, with two cows and a bull and a lot of pure cussedness. We didn't always have a lot to eat, but we didn't starve. I went to school, and did the chores early in the morning and after school. When I was ten, he legally adopted me, so I could have his name. It was the name I'd always used, but it wasn't my legal name. There wasn't any fuss about it; no one knew where my mother was, and my grandparents were getting on in years. They weren't able to take in and handle a ten-year-old hellion, which is what I was.''

Tessa continued stroking his hair long after he stopped talking. No wonder he was so aloof, his emotions so controlled! In all his life, there had been only one person he could rely on. He had spent his earliest years leading a transient way of life, with people and places merely stops along the way. His only constant was his father, yet he would have seen that other children had two parents, with a doting mother and a stable homelife, while his own mother had given him away. He had grown up wary, not allowing anyone to get close to him, because the only person he felt able to trust was his father.

Given his childhood, was it any surprise that he hadn't automatically trusted her? Understanding began to ease her mind, bringing her a measure of peace, though even now she didn't know if she'd ever be able to forgive him. Her fingers sifted through his hair. If only she didn't love him so much!

He lifted himself on his elbow, allowing himself access to her breasts, and his hard fingers moved gently over her soft curves, coaxing her velvety nipples into taut little nubs. "When Tom meets you, he's going to melt into a little puddle on the ground. He's got an uncontrollable weakness when it comes to women, anyway, and he's going to fall in love with my delicious little Southern belle." There was a huskier note in his voice now, and he bent his head to suck leisurely at her excited flesh.

Tessa whimpered at the sudden pleasure that jolted her body. He rolled her nipple around with his tongue, then lifted his head to run his hand over her breast in patent satisfaction. "You're well blessed, as delicate as you are. Your bones are so slim I sometimes feel as if I could snap you in two. But here..." He chuckled richly.

Tessa blushed hotly in the darkness; then he put his mouth on her breasts again and it no longer mattered.

She slept afterward, but soon he woke her to love her again. The rest of the night was like that, with him returning to her time and again, demonstrating to her with his body how much he wanted her. She knew that was his purpose, but she needed that intense attention to boost her self-esteem, to restore her faith in her own femininity, and he devoted himself passionately to that goal.

When she woke for the last time to a brightly sunny day, it was to find him propped on his elbow over her, watching her sleep. Dark stubble roughened his jaw, making him look like a roughneck, but his face bore the relaxation of complete physical contentment. He knew what the hours of his lovemaking had done for her, and his satisfaction was plain in his eyes. Their gazes met, and locked.

"Good morning," he murmured, pushing a strand of hair from her eyes.

She yawned, stretching under his appreciative gaze. "Good morning. Aren't you late for work?"

"I'm not going to work. This part is all up to Evan and Sammy. My part is staying here with you and keeping you satisfied."

She regarded him somberly; she was more sensitive now to everything about him, and she knew he was being evasive. "I promise you I won't bolt. Is that what you're afraid of?"

"The thought occurred to me."

"I'm still confused," she said slowly. "I don't know what to do, but last night...I did a lot of thinking. I still love you, and after hearing all the evidence that pointed to me, I can't blame you for thinking that I took that money. What else could you think? I still can't...I can't quite forgive you, but I can't walk away from you, either."

His face tightened at her words. "I won't let you walk away. Give us time; that's all I'm asking."

"All right. I can afford the time; I don't have anything else to do," she said with a residue of bitterness.

He swung off the bed and restlessly swiped his pants up from the floor, where he'd left them the night before. "Do you want to go back to work?" he asked sharply.

"At Carter Engineering? No, I don't think so, not after this. But I'll have to go to work somewhere, won't I? I have the normal assortment of bills to pay."

"Do me a favor. Don't look for anything yet."

"Why shouldn't I?"

He sighed, thrusting his hand through his hair. "Because we won't be living here."

She got out of bed, too, and put her robe on. "Aren't you taking a lot for granted?" she asked quietly.

"Not as much as I want to," he assured her in a grim tone. "Just don't look for work yet. You don't have to worry about money; I'll take care of everything—and don't get your back up at me, you little wildcat. You've been through a rough time and you need a sort of emotional vacation. And since I've moved in on you, it's only fair that I pay my way."

"You're trying to make me dependent on you."

"Is that so bad? Honey, we're trying to work our way through a rough patch. A lack of trust is what caused the problem to begin with. Let's trust each other for a change, emotionally as well as physically."

"For how long? When do you have to go back to San Francisco?"

His face went abruptly blank, and she could read nothing in that expressionless mask. "There's no rush."

His very calmness alarmed her, and she twisted the ties to her robe. "Evan said you could be fired. Is that it?"

"No. I haven't been fired. You don't have to worry about my job, honey."

There was something he wasn't telling her, but his gaze was so deliberately bland that she knew she would be wasting her time trying to pry the information out of him. How was she supposed to trust him when he was still hiding things from her? Frustrated at the way she kept running into an emotional dead end, she turned away abruptly. "I'm going to take a shower."

"That sounds...interesting," he drawled. "I was going to take one myself."

"Fine. You can have the bathroom when I'm finished."

Still naked, totally relaxed, he watched her gather her underwear. "I take it that I'm not invited." He made the words a statement rather than a question.

"No, you're not. It won't take me long. Why don't you start breakfast? Then I'll take over and you can shower. It should be ready by the time you're finished."

He gave in easily. "All right, if that's what you want."

"It is."

She was uneasy, wondering if he might join her anyway, but he was as good as his word. When she left the shower she smelled the delightful aroma of fresh coffee, and the scent made her realize how hungry she was. She dressed hurriedly, then rushed to the kitchen to take over the breakfast preparations. She stopped in the doorway, momentarily stunned at having a tall, powerfully muscled man standing stark naked in her kitchen, whistling through his teeth as he assembled the ingredients for pancakes.

"Why didn't you put on some clothes?" she asked weakly.

"Just letting you get a good look at what you turned down," he explained with dead-level calm as he walked past her.

He'd done that, all right. Her palms were moist, her breathing a little fast, as she mixed the pancake batter and poured it in small circles on the grill. He knew exactly what he'd done to her, because he had taught her, trained her responses until his lightest touch could arouse her.

Right on time, he came back into the kitchen, decently attired in jeans and an open-necked shirt, but still the sight of him made her mouth go dry. He had certainly known what he was doing by moving in with her, she thought dimly. He probably planned on keeping her so drunk on sex that she'd do anything he wanted.

She tensed as she realized what she was thinking. She was automatically attributing ulterior motives to his actions, rather than making an effort to trust him. But you couldn't just make an arbitrary decision to start trusting someone; trust had to be learned, and earned. He had taken very good care of her, and with his love-making he had gone a long way toward helping her recover her equilibrium, but a part of her remained wary of him. She didn't want it to be that way. She wanted to simply walk into his arms and forget everything that had happened, but she just couldn't do it. She was still afraid.

"Eat," he said gently, making her realize that she was sitting at the table with her fork motionless in her hand.

"I can't decide," she explained in a low tone, and he knew exactly what she was talking about.

"You don't have to decide now. We have time. Let it ride."

"I do love you," she said achingly.

"I know," he said.

He was restless after they had cleaned the dishes, and he prowled around her small apartment. Several times she started to suggest that he go to work, since he was obviously bored, but there was a growing edge to his temper that made her reluctant to suggest anything to him. She had been depressed and listless, and had let her normal chores slide, but her old energy was back, and she had plenty to do in cleaning and catching up on her laundry, so she generally ignored him and let him prowl. When the telephone rang early in the afternoon, and he leaped for it, she suddenly realized that he'd been waiting for the call.

Hurrying to his side, she tried to piece together the conversation from his noncommittal responses, but he was a master at one-word answers. His eyes were flinty, his mouth a hard line as he listened.

"Okay. I'll be right there," he said, and hung up.

"What is it?" she asked anxiously, dogging his footsteps as he went into the bedroom and began pulling off his clothes. "Have they found out who did it?"

"Maybe," he grunted. He was in slacks and a dress shirt before she realized that he wasn't going to tell her anything else, and as he began capably knotting a tie around his neck, her brows snapped together.

"Oh, no you don't, Brett Rutland! You're not leaving me here without telling me anything!" She kicked off her shoes and wiggled out of her jeans. "I'm coming with you."

"No, you're not." He hooked his jacket over one finger and seized her by the nape of the neck, holding her still while he bent and kissed her roughly. "It could get dirty, and I don't want you hurt, not any more than you already have been. See you later."

"Brett!" she yelled furiously at his back, and her voice cracked.

He stopped at the door and looked over his shoulder at her. For the first time, she saw the murderous look in his eyes, and she shivered, suddenly glad that that look wasn't directed at her. "I'll be back," he said evenly.

The apartment was silent and empty without him, and her nerves crawled when she remembered the way he had looked. If that look had been meant for her, she'd have died of fright on the spot. He was always controlled. She couldn't imagine him in a rage, yet she sensed that he had been holding on to his control by only the narrowest of margins. He knew who had done the embezzling, who had deliberately blamed it on her, but he hadn't told her. Who could have done it, that he would hesitate to reveal the embezzler's identity to her? Someone she trusted?

She had been too frightened to really wonder about the identity of the criminal, even though she realized the necessity of discovering who it had been. Whoever it was had to hate her, and again Tessa's conception of herself was shaken. What had she done to deserve such hatred, such vindictiveness?

Her thoughts tumbled about like a mad squirrel, trying to recall every woman who worked at Carter Engineering, trying desperately to think of something she had done, but nothing came to mind. She hadn't stolen anyone's lover, or broken up a relationship. She couldn't remember doing anything that would earn her an enemy, yet she had.

Tortured by her inability to find a reason for what had happened, she began to cry, soft, soundless sobs that were full of misery. Where was Brett when she needed him? Didn't he know how painful it was to be so totally in the dark? No, how could he know? Brett had never been in the dark; he was always in control, always on top of the situation. She had reached out to him during the night trying, almost in spite of herself, to mend the rift between them. She loved him; she wanted to trust him with her love, and she wanted to be certain that he loved her in return. Yet he had left her alone with her thoughts, knowing that she must be wild with anxiety and uncertainty. Was that love? Had he walked out to give her the chance to make her decision, taking the chance that, when he returned, she wouldn't be there?

The afternoon became night, and Tessa's nerves were so jittery that she jumped and stifled a small cry when a key turned in the lock and Brett entered, his face tired and lined. Sammy was with him, looking as pale and tired as Tessa felt, but his presence barely registered on her consciousness. She stared at the key in Brett's hand. "You took my house key," she said numbly.

He looked at the key in his hand and grimaced. "Yeah," he said, putting the key back into his pocket. Coming over to her, he looked down at her critically, examining every inch of her. "You've been crying again, damn it," he said fiercely.

"Did you...find out anything?"

Instead of answering, Brett asked, "Is there any fresh coffee? I need something to keep me going."

"No, there isn't. Brett, answer me!"

"I'll make a pot."

She stormed to her feet. "I'm going to throw the pot at you if you don't answer my question!"

An unwilling grin twisted his mouth and brought a gleam to his eyes. "Hellcat," he said with tender affection. "Sammy is going to tell you what's going on."

Tessa whirled on Sammy, who stood with his hands shoved deep into his pockets. His blue eyes were miserable. "It's my fault," he said grimly. He had always seemed so boyish, even though he was older than she, but he looked as if he had aged ten years overnight.

She shook her head. That didn't make any sense at all. "How could it be your fault? You're not the embezzler."

"It's Hillary. She did it for me."

It was as if someone had drawn a curtain aside. Tessa stared at him in horrified realization, immediately seeing the whole of it. All of it was there. Poor Hillary, so shy and unsure of herself, and so much in love with Sammy. Sammy had needed money to develop his electronic ideas; Hillary had gotten it for him. She had had all the opportunity she could want: She worked in a bank; she worked with Sammy, and through him had access to the computers at Carter Engineering; and she was smart enough to know how to do it. Even choosing Tessa as the scapegoat made sense, because Sammy so obviously admired Tessa, because Tessa was bright and charming and confident, relaxed with men, while Hillary froze with shyness.

She looked at Sammy, her eyes brimming with sympathetic tears.

"I traced it," he said hoarsely. "She accessed the computer several times from my apartment. She has a key.... She came and went anytime she wanted. My God, I practically set it up for her! Tessa, I traced it back to my own number!"

He was shaking; she went to him and put her arms around him, and they clung together. "What happened?" she whispered, aching for him.

"We met her when she got off work at the bank, Mr. Rutland and Evan and I. She saw us and just...started crying. She knew."

"Has he had her arrested yet?" Tessa asked shakily.

"No, I haven't. I wanted to talk to you first," Brett interrupted coolly. He had been leaning, unnoticed, in the doorway. Now he straightened and walked over to Tessa. "My first instinct is to lock her away, for what she did to you more than for taking the money. But I don't want revenge to be my motive for doing anything, so everything's on hold. Evan is with her now, babysitting and waiting for my call."

Appalled, Tessa stared at him. He was asking her to decide the fate of another human being. It was up to her whether he prosecuted Hillary, or let her go. Why was he so certain that revenge wouldn't color *her* thinking? She was human, too! "Brett, don't do this to me."

"I know what I'm asking," he said flatly, not taking his eyes from her. "But you see, baby, I trust your judgment."

Chapter Eleven

Tessa trembled all over as she stood there staring at him, her eyes begging him. She was hurting, he knew; she was acutely sensitive now, reacting to every nuance in the air. This had changed her. Where before she had been effervescent, sparkling like a vintage champagne, now she was quieter, the laughter stilled. He hoped it hadn't gone forever. The charm of that joyous laughter had been what first lured him, yet he loved her anyway; he loved the woman, and her gift of joyousness had been only a part of the reason why he loved her. If she gave him the chance, he intended to devote his life to bringing that sparkle back into her eyes, but first he had to get over the agony of a decision that was only hers to make. Not even Joshua Carter's interest in this matched Tessa's because she was the one who had suffered the most.

"Let her go," she said.

Her voice was faint, but Brett heard her. He went to her and put his hand on her arm, steadying her. "Are you sure?"

Tessa nodded, and Brett eased her down onto the couch. Sammy dropped into a chair as if he'd suddenly gone boneless, and maybe he had.

She clutched at Brett's hands, holding them as if they were lifelines. "Hillary loves him. She did it because she loves him. I can understand that, because I'd go to any lengths for you—" She broke off, afraid that she was saying too much, but her shaky, tumbling words were all he'd hoped to hear, and more. He had the feeling that Tessa did understand, that she knew more than they did, even though she had been told only the bare bones of it.

Tessa looked desperately at Sammy. "Sammy, she loves you. You know that, don't you?"

He looked stunned and exhausted. "I can't take it in. She didn't have any reason to be jealous of you! If anything, you were always trying to get us together."

"But she didn't know that, did she? And that's only part of it. She believed in you, in what you were doing."

"Chewing on it won't do any good," Brett said quietly, the authority in his voice making both of them fall silent. "And wallowing in guilt won't do any good, either. I know. I've already tried it. What we have to do now is work out a solution that Mr. Carter will accept. He's due total reimbursement, if nothing else. The money has been spent. What do you suggest?''

Sammy chewed on his lip. "Nelda is marketable. I've thought of selling her to a computer company, but if that won't work..."

"If you say the computer is marketable, I'll take your word on it. Since you had already planned to sell it anyway, I don't feel that we'll be taking anything away from you, except the amount of money that was stolen."

Relief was plain on Sammy's face. "Do you mean it? It won't be any more complicated than that?"

"It'll be complicated by the time a lawyer gets through with it," Brett said dryly. "And I can't promise that Mr. Carter will go for it, though I think he will. It's the same terms I twisted his arm to get for Tessa, so he shouldn't kick too much about it."

"Will it take very long to get it settled?"

"Nelda will have to be sold, and that could take some time, because you'll want to wait for the best offer, but the legal paperwork won't take that long."

Leaving Tessa, he walked Sammy to the door. Tessa was watching them, and she saw the worried frown on Sammy's face. "I don't know what to do about Hillary," he muttered. "I was trying to get up enough nerve to ask her to marry me, but now..."

"Do what I was going to do," Brett advised sharply. "Put her over your knee and whale the living daylights out of her. That's the least of what she deserves."

He closed the door on Sammy and came back to Tessa's side. He was tenderness itself as he sat down beside her and hugged her against him, his eyes worried. Gently he brushed her hair back from her forehead. "Are you all right? It's over now, really over."

She didn't feel as if *finis* had been written to the episode; when she looked at him, she knew that there were still problems to be solved, but now didn't seem to be the time to go into them. "You don't have to treat me like china," she said with a faint smile. "It was a shock, but I'm not going to break."

"I hated to do that to you, but I couldn't trust myself to make a rational decision. No matter which way I went, I knew I'd always doubt my reasons for doing it."

"And if I had wanted her prosecuted?"

The hard, flinty expression came back into his eyes. "You would have wanted what I wanted."

He was a little frightening, a hard man who wouldn't tolerate any threat against anything or anyone he considered his. The realization, instead of frightening her, made her eyes widen. He felt that way about her. It wasn't guilt, but an expression of something she had sensed the first time he had made love to her. The act had not been one of casual pleasure, but one of possession, in the most basic way. She had become his, which was why he had lashed out at her when he thought she had betrayed him and his trust. Yet even before he knew her to be innocent, he had begun working for her release. Her innocence or guilt hadn't mattered; she was his, and he would have handled it. That was why he had given Sammy that rather primitive advice.

"Were you going to beat me?" she asked, giving him a hard look.

He made no apologies. "I was planning on it. I doubt I'd ever have done it, because I couldn't deliberately hurt you, but thinking about it made me feel better. Now, with Sammy...that girl may get the spanking of her life. When the quiet ones get angry, there's no stopping them. Do you care? Are you really that forgiving?"

"No, I'm not. I'm far more human than that," she replied with a flash of spirit. "I'd like to punch her out. But this has gone on long enough, and I want it to end. Let Sammy take care of her. I just want to put it behind me and forget about it. Besides, if you had prosecuted, Sammy would have been hurt, too, and he didn't deserve it."

He gave a soft sigh, and removed his arm from around her, leaving her feeling faintly chilled. His expression was grim as he leaned forward, resting his forearms on his thighs. "If you're so generous with a stranger, why can't you be that generous with me? Why can't you forgive me and give me a second chance? I'm not asking for time, but for a real second chance." He drew a deep breath, waiting for her reaction.

Tessa stared at him, stricken by what he had said, because it was nothing less than the truth. She *had* been more generous with a stranger than she had been with him, and she loved him more than she'd ever thought it was possible to love anyone or anything. But precisely because she did love him so much, his lack of trust had cut her far more deeply than Hillary's treacherous actions. Hillary didn't mean anything to her at all, except as someone important to one of her friends.

So this was love, she thought painfully. It wasn't only forgiving, it was taking a chance that her love was returned. He had lashed out at her only when he thought she'd betrayed him first, and even then, when his first pain had faded, he had moved swiftly to protect her. Even thinking that she was guilty, he had forgiven her and reached out for her.

It was love, and she really didn't have a choice about trusting him, because she had no life without him.

She had been silent for a long time, and Brett's mouth had firmed into a grim line. He had one more card to play, one more chance at convincing her that he loved her, that he'd do whatever he had to do to protect her. If she misunderstood his motives now, he didn't know what he would do, because he was playing his last card. "Tessa, I've resigned my job."

She made a sharp movement, and the color washed out of her face. "But...but you told me that you didn't have to worry about your job!"

"I don't. Because I don't have one. I resigned Monday, effective whenever this was finished. The deal I made with Joshua," he said carefully, "was that in exchange for you, I would continue to do the occasional consulting job for him. That's what he called it, anyway. It means I'll get the easy jobs like negotiating the settlement of a strike, or industrial espionage, things like that. But for the most part, I intend to be on the ranch with you, raising kids and cattle."

Her heart was doing crazy things in her chest, interfering with her breathing. "Is that a proposal?" she demanded.

"I guess it is. I intend to be the father of your children, and I'd like for it to be legal." His entire world hinged on her answer, and he couldn't read her expression at all. He started to sweat. "Do you love me enough to forgive me?"

She got to her feet, propelled by a sudden need for action, anything to give herself something to do. "It was never a matter of forgiving," she said jerkily. "I love you so much I think I can forgive you anything. That doesn't mean I'd let you get away with it," she added, in case he got the wrong idea. "It just means I'd forgive you for it."

Something was changing in his face; his navy eyes were lighting, as if fired from the inside. "After you threw hot lemonade on me? Or hit me over the head with something?"

"Or kicked you out of our bed."

"Whoa, honey, you're talking nasty now. If there's one place I'm going to be, it's in bed with you. But if you forgive me, what was the problem?"

"I was trying to decide if I should take you without being sure you loved me, or wait until I was sure," she said baldly.

He surged to his feet, towering over her, his shoulders so broad that they blocked out the light. "Would you like a demonstration of what it's like to be a rancher's wife?"

Suddenly she was the old Tessa again, her long lashes sweeping down languidly to hide the vibrant sparkle in her green eyes. "Why, I believe I would," she said in her slowest, most wicked drawl, the one that made Brett's loins turn to molten lava. With a low growl, he tossed her over his shoulder and carried her off to bed.

Some men didn't know when they were well off, he thought an hour later. She was turning the charm on him, enticing him and teasing him and generally driving him crazy, and even though he knew he was being managed, there wasn't a damn thing he could do to help himself.

She lay propped above him, her lovely breasts nestled into the hair that covered his chest and doing a good job of distracting him. She was winding one finger through the curls of hair, then she moved it on to his ear, his mouth, his throat, across his shoulder and down his arm, over to his side, down his hip.... What she did with that one finger was amazing. He shifted restlessly, considering tossing her over on her back and finishing what she'd started, but she was still talking.

"I want to get married in Tennessee," she murmured, nipping at his chin with her white teeth, then kissing the slight sting away. "In our old church in Sevierville, with Aunt Silver there. You do want your father to be best man, don't you?"

"I don't care," he muttered in raw frustration, sitting up abruptly and dumping her off his chest. As he reached for her she drew away, but she caught his hand and carried his fingers to her lips, where she nibbled and sucked at each of his fingertips in turn.

Her voice was dreamy. "I want to show you the farm, and the old country roads. Gatlinburg is best in the spring and summer, I think. We can go into all the old-time crafts stores on Glades Road, and walk in the mountains. I want to show you the whole park. We can go to the Chimneys, and Cade's Cove, and Grandfather Mountain. And I want to see *Unto These Hills* one last time—"

He put his hand over her mouth, stifling the flow of words. "Tessa, darling, *yes*! I'll agree to anything you want. I'll marry you anywhere you want, in front of as many people as you want, and I'll hike from Tennessee to Wyoming with you, if that's what you want. Now, does that cover everything?"

A suspicious sound came from behind his hand, and he looked into green eyes that were brimming with laughter, sparkling in the way that he loved. She'd been playing with him, he realized, deliberately driving him mad with frustration, and loving her feminine power to do so. If he hadn't been so certain of her intention of fully satisfying him, he'd have erupted into rage, but all he could do was fall back on the bed, his chest heaving with his heavy breathing.

He'd asked for it. She was just what he wanted, every devilish, delicious inch of her. He had to be crazy, considering what a chase she was going to lead him on for the rest of their lives. Then he chuckled, and before she could evade him again, he had reached out a brawny arm and toppled her onto the bed. Quickly he covered her, parting her legs and taking her. "This is what you get for teasing me," he said, kissing her hungrily.

An expression of delight spread across her lovely, exotic face, radiant now with his love. "Really?" she drawled. "Oh, good."

The moonlight spilled across the big bed, lighting a room with polished wooden floors covered by a hand-woven rug. The bed was long and wide, big enough to accommodate the length of the man who sprawled in it. Tessa sat up in the bed, folding her arms and resting them on top of her knees, and putting her chin on top of her arms. They had been married only that morning, and Brett had barely given her time to pack before he'd whisked her to Knoxville to catch a plane. She had hugged Aunt Silver and cried, knowing that this time she was truly leaving. Her home would be in Wyoming now, not in Tennessee. Silver had cried, too, until Tom, Brett's father, had snatched her up in his brawny arms and kissed her until she'd forgotten about crying.

"Come visit," he'd growled to the astonished woman in his arms. "I'd love to have you." His deep voice had given the words another meaning, probably his real meaning, because Tom was a big, hard, battle-scarred old tomcat of a man.

The flight had been a long one, from Knoxville to Chicago to Denver, then to Cheyenne, and they had flown the last leg of the journey in their own plane. By then Tessa had been exhausted, curled up in her seat sound asleep. Brett had shaken her awake only when the plane was on the ground at the ranch. The drive from the dirt airstrip to the ranch house had been a short one, but she'd been fully awake by the time they reached the house. Brett had carried her inside and straight up to his room, and a grinning Tom had brought their suitcases in.

"We have a private bathroom," Brett had said, opening a door off the bedroom. "Are you hungry, or would you rather take a bath and go to bed?"

Tessa had stretched and yawned. "Why don't I take a bath, then get something to eat, then go to bed? How does that sound?"

"Too damned long," he muttered. He looked longingly at the big bed.

"Poor baby, are you tired?" she'd purred.

"No."

"Hungry?"

"Yes."

It had been obvious that her man wasn't concerned with his stomach. She had slowly unbuttoned her blouse and drawn it off, then unhooked her bra and dropped it. "Why don't you take a shower with me?" she'd suggested innocently. "That would save time."

His eyes had narrowed, and his hands had gone to the buttons of his shirt. "I hope you're not really hungry, darling, because it could be a while before you have dinner. As a matter of fact, we'll probably have to call it breakfast."

"You can take me down for a midnight snack," she had said, stepping out of her skirt.

"Deal."

Now she really was hungry, and it was long after midnight. His hand touched her back, but she wasn't startled. Gently his long fingers moved down her spine.

"I fantasized about this, the first night I made love to you." His smoky, whiskey-rough voice was low, and it rubbed over her like a caress. "I held you after you'd gone to sleep, and I thought of how it would be to make love to you in this bed, and hold you when the loving was finished. I decided then that I was going to marry you."

She turned and went into his arms, rubbing her face into the hair on his chest. "Was it as good as your fantasy?"

He laughed. "It was better. You were awake this time."

"Good enough that you'd like to do it again?"

"Now, that's a foolish question if I've ever heard one."

"There's a purpose to it. I was about to point out that if you want to keep my strength up, you're going to have to feed me."

"All right, Mrs. Rutland, hint taken." He got out of bed and pulled on his pants. He began zipping them, then looked up at her as she tried to straighten the tangle of her nightgown. Even in the moonlight he could tell that her lips were sweetly swollen, her hair mussed. She wore the look of a woman in love, and a woman who had been thoroughly loved.

"I'm glad you're my wife," he said simply.

Tessa discarded the nightgown and made do with her robe, tying the belt securely around her slender waist. "I am, too," she said, and went into his arms. The horrible, nightmarish week was gone now, in the past where it belonged. She had changed, yes, but so had he. They had both let their barriers down, because there was no room for barriers between them. How could she not trust this man? Not only was her life safe in his hands, but also her love.

READERS' COMMENTS ON SILHOUETTE SPECIAL EDITIONS:

"I just finished reading the first six Silhouette Special Edition Books and I had to take the opportunity to write you and tell you how much I enjoyed them. I enjoyed all the authors in this series. Best wishes on your Silhouette Special Editions line and many thanks."

—B.H.*, Jackson, OH

"The Special Editions are really special and I enjoyed them very much! I am looking forward to next month's books."

—R.M.W.*, Melbourne, FL

"I've just finished reading four of your first six Special Editions and I enjoyed them very much. I like the more sensual detail and longer stories. I will look forward each month to your new Special Editions."

—L.S.*, Visalia, CA

"Silhouette Special Editions are — 1.) Superb! 2.) Great! 3.) Delicious! 4.) Fantastic! . . . Did I leave anything out? These are books that an adult woman can read . . . I love them!"

—H.C.*, Monterey Park, CA

*names available on request

Silhouette Special Edition

COMING NEXT MONTH

THE HEART'S YEARNING—Ginna Gray
When Laura's search for the son she'd had to give up finally ended, she was content to watch him from afar…until Adam Kincaid, her son's adoptive father, unwittingly drew her into a triangle of love.

STAR-CROSSED—Ruth Langan
Fiercely protective Adam London was determined to stop B.J. Conover from writing his mother's biography, but B.J. had a job to do and she couldn't let her growing feelings for Adam stand in her way.

A PERFECT VISION—Monica Barrie
Architect Lea Graham envisioned a community nestled in the New Mexican landscape that Darren Laird was determined to preserve. Could the love that they shared survive a fight to the finish to save their separate dreams?

MEMORIES OF THE HEART—Jean Kent
Was it really possible that foundling Suzy Yoder was the long-lost Hepburn baby, heiress to a vast fortune? Attorney Rich Link had to find the answer, for reasons both legal and personal.

AUTUMN RECKONING—Maggi Charles
Deep in the Berkshire mountains, Marc Bouchard fell in love. Children's-book author Jennifer Bently was more than she'd led him to believe, and her deception threatened the love that they had dared to share.

ODDS AGAINST TOMORROW—Patti Beckman
Every jockey dreams of winning the Kentucky Derby, but for jockey Nikki Cameron the stakes were almost too high. If she triumphed on the bluegrass track, she risked losing the only man she'd ever loved.

AVAILABLE NOW:

ONE MAN'S ART
Nora Roberts

THE CUTTING EDGE
Linda Howard

SECOND GENERATION
Roslyn MacDonald

EARTH AND FIRE
Jennifer West

JUST ANOTHER PRETTY FACE
Elaine Camp

MIDNIGHT SUN
Lisa Jackson